A Day at the Beach Hut

Also by Veronica Henry

Wild Oats
An Eligible Bachelor
Love on the Rocks
Marriage and Other Games
The Beach Hut
The Birthday Party
The Long Weekend
A Night on the Orient Express
The Beach Hut Next Door
High Tide
How to Find Love in a Book Shop
The Forever House
A Family Recipe
Christmas at the Beach Hut
A Home from Home
A Wedding at the Beach Hut

THE HONEYCOTE NOVELS

A Country Christmas
(*previously published as* Honeycote)

A Country Life
(*previously published as* Making Hay)

A Country Wedding
(*previously published as* Just a Family Affair)

A Day at the Beach Hut

Stories and recipes
inspired by seaside life

VERONICA HENRY

with illustrations by Sarah Corbett

ORION

First published in Great Britain in 2021 by Orion Fiction,
an imprint of The Orion Publishing Group Ltd
Carmelite House, 50 Victoria Embankment,
London EC4Y 0DZ

An Hachette UK company

1 3 5 7 9 10 8 6 4 2

A CIP catalogue record for this book is
available from the British Library.

ISBN (Mass Market Paperback) 978 1 4091 9581 8
ISBN (eBook) 978 1 4091 9582 5

Printed and bound in Great Britain
by Clays Ltd, Elcograf, S.p.A

To the Cadhay Crew

For never-ending support and laughter and
love of food and words

Daniel, Heidi, Helen, Katy, Lexi, Lucy,
Marcia, Matt, Pam A, Pam L, Sue and Vicky

CONTENTS

INTRODUCTION

Just over ten years ago, I was driving down the long and winding hill that leads from the lighthouse where I'd just walked my dog, Zelda. It was sometime after Easter but before the May bank holiday – when you're a writer, the days and weeks and months merge into one, punctuated only by deadlines and publications, so dates are always a bit of a blur.

The sun was shining, my window was down and the Eagles were telling me they'd got a peaceful, easy feeling – and so had I. To my right, the sea sparkled and the waves flirted with the rocks and there were a few silly clouds scudding about as if imitating the sheep scattered below. And then I rounded the corner and I could see the curve of the beach in front of me, pink sand glittering, and my heart skipped a beat.

For there they were. A band of workmen had sneaked in over the past few days with their diggers and trucks and tools, shifting the sands to build a sturdy bank. And on that bank was a line of beach huts, newly painted and gleaming red, yellow, blue and green, each one with a girl's name stencilled over the door – Jemima, Rosemary, Gertrude, Edith …

And this little row of seventy huts told me more than anything that summer was on its way; more than the citric swathes of gorse on the hills, the frothy heads of cow parsley in the hedges, the persistently loud and inconsiderate dawn chorus that woke me each morning.

With the huts' arrival the rest of the village stretched its arms and came to life: the surfboards were propped up on the pavements, the chip shop took delivery of tons of potatoes, the freezers were filled with ice creams, the pasties put in to bake.

As I looked down on the huts from my vantage point, I had one of those lightbulb moments.

An idea floated into my mind on the sea breeze: a novel that was effectively a series of short stories, each one set in a different beach hut with different characters but who were all joined together by the location …

I emailed my publisher.

'Stop what you're doing and write it now,' she commanded.

Less than a year later *The Beach Hut* was published. Now I've written four novels and a Quick Reads novella set in the same fictional location – Everdene – and I've had hundreds of letters and messages and emails from people all saying the same thing: how much they long for a beach hut of their own.

Like a caravan or a shed on an allotment, a beach hut is somewhere one can simply *be*. They are reminiscent of Thermos flasks full of cocoa, Tupperware boxes crammed with sandwiches, of doing jigsaw puzzles while the rain thrums on the roof. Rock pools, sandcastles and 99 ice creams.

After a horribly difficult year in 2020 and now into 2021, we have all been craving comfort and security, somewhere safe and familiar yet also offering an escape from everyday life, somewhere we can relax with family or friends or a lover. The call of the sea has never been stronger, and there has been a return to the simpler things in life, a need to tune in to nature and the elements. And, of course, the joy of eating together has become more important: something we no longer take for granted but instead treasure.

And so I've decided to return to my fictional beach huts once again, but this time I've put a little spin on it. There's a fresh catch of stories, taking you from dawn till dusk on a summer's day on Everdene Sands, each accompanied by my favourite recipes.

Because for me one of the pleasures of time spent at the beach is the food, whether it's the perfect egg sandwich oozing mayonnaise, a wrap of scalding-hot chips eaten on the harbour wall, fuggy with vinegar, or the day's catch thrown onto the barbecue. Sea air sharpens the appetite and the simplest things become a feast. Over the years I have conjured up hundreds of meals for my family and friends, from fat sausages stuffed into a floury roll to a lavish seafood birthday banquet. These recipes are the mainstays of beach hut life: hearty breakfasts to sustain a day's surfing, easily transportable picnic food and simple suppers to restore flagging energy at the end of the day.

This little book will transport you straight to the dunes, the marram grass slapping at your legs, your picnic basket filled with delicious treats. Or take you down to the harbour to watch the boats come in and land the day's haul, gulls swooping overhead, eyes beady with greed. Or settle you down to watch a pinky-orange sun fall behind the horizon, turning the sea to molten copper.

I hope you enjoy your day at the beach hut.

Veronica

Breakfast

The Early Bird

'If you're not up to it this year, honestly don't worry,' her daughter-in-law said a week before they were due to arrive, and Elspeth's heart had leapt into her mouth. Was this Melanie's way of saying the children didn't want to come? Elspeth quite understood why they wouldn't. At seventeen, fifteen and thirteen, why would three teenagers want to spend a week cooped up by the sea with their grandmother? They had far more interesting things to do in the streets of London, she was sure. Friends to meet, shops to go to, computer games to play. There was no wi-fi at the beach hut. Not even a telly. None of the mod cons that sustained the young.

She certainly didn't want them to feel obliged to spend time with her.

'If they've got other things on, I quite understand.'

'No! They're dying to come,' Melanie assured her. 'But not if it's too much for you. I mean, it's very soon …'

'It's not too much at all.' Elspeth didn't want to reveal how much she was longing to see them. She'd had enough of her own company. People had been wonderful, but after the initial flurry that always comes after a bereavement, the phone calls and visits had slowed to a trickle. And now that she had decamped to Everdene for the summer, there was no one to call in. The neighbours in the huts around her had gradually changed over the years. It wasn't the old set. There was hardly anyone her age here. Barely anyone she knew.

'Well, you make sure they pull their weight,' Melanie was saying. 'If you're absolutely sure, I'll bring them down this Saturday.'

'Wonderful.' The relief was honey-sweet. She didn't know what she would have done if they hadn't come. The disappointment would have been overwhelming, though she would never have let on. Stoic to the end, was Elspeth. She never complained. No one liked a whinger. Just get on with it, was her motto, and it had served her well.

And now, here they all were: Harry, Edward and Meg, crammed like sardines into the hut. They'd arrived late last night in an adolescent whirl of headphones, sunglasses, trainers and rucksacks, smelling of hair gel and sweet perfume. They didn't seem to mind the mismatched arrangement of bunks and camp beds and put-you-ups. They'd brought their own duvets and pillows and were snuggled up, still fast asleep. Elspeth was always awake

8

at dawn, and she loved lying in her bed, feeling their presence as the sun came up.

'You'll be lucky to see them before lunchtime,' Melanie had warned when she'd dropped them, rolling her eyes.

Elspeth didn't mind how long they slept. She was grateful for the sound of their breathing, the beating of their hearts. Some of the blood pumping round their bodies was hers, and that felt comforting. And some was Harry's, too, which made him feel a little nearer ... Her husband Harry, who their oldest grandchild had been named after. Would she ever get used to losing him?

They'd had fish and chips last night, because that was the tradition. They always had them on the first night and the last night. The scent of cod and vinegar still lingered, mixed in with the salty air from outside as she opened the door. It looked set to be a beautiful day: still chilly, with the kind of snappy breeze that set washing dancing on the line, the sun still uncertain, but promising to gain in confidence as the day went on.

She would head out for provisions. She knew from experience there was no point in stocking up in advance. She had to shop every day, for the three of them would eat every scrap available; as much as she bought, they would devour. She went over to her oldest grandchild, fast asleep under a duvet covered in a smattering of dinosaurs left over from childhood. She tapped him on the arm.

Harry's eyes flew open and he half rose up, looking

9

at her in alarm. His russet hair was dishevelled, his skin milk-pale that would soon turn gold after a week. His shoulders were broad now, his brows thicker, his voice deep. Elspeth's heart twisted with love for her grandson, the spit of the grandfather he was named for. He had read a poem at the funeral and Elspeth had never been so proud.

'I'm popping to the farm shop for breakfast things,' she whispered. 'I'll be about an hour.'

He nodded, his eyelids drooping almost immediately as he fell back onto his pillow. He was asleep again straight away, and she wondered if he would remember her message. It didn't much matter. They wouldn't panic if they found her gone. They weren't panicky children. They were at home here. There was tea, and milk, and a box of cornflakes if they were really starving.

She pulled on her shorts and a t-shirt and her walking boots, looking critically at her legs, speckled and lumpy; mapped with ugly veins. Once they had been smooth, the colour of butterscotch, and she had shown them off under the white seersucker tennis dress she had made herself, a dark-haired girl with laughing eyes who had won the singles trophy for three summers in a row at school.

And the tennis had stood her in good stead. She'd met Harry during her first summer at university, playing opposite him at mixed doubles. She couldn't take her eyes off his lean, rangy body; the hair that fell over his eyes; the gold of his skin. His backhand was formidable but she hit it back every time, with equal force, to get his attention. And it worked ...

She rummaged among the coats and waterproofs on the coat hook for her rucksack. It was far easier to carry things on her back, she had learned. Of course, the easiest thing to do would have been to walk up past the rest of the beach huts to the village and go to the mini market, but if grief had taught her anything it was to do things the hard way. It made time pass much more quickly. And she needed the walk. It had become her medicine, the steep climb that made her legs ache and her heart pound.

So instead she turned left and walked to the far end of the line of huts on Everdene Sands, then up the dunes. It was always hard to get purchase as the sand made you slip downwards, but she had perfected her method, stepping in other people's footprints until she reached the dirt track at the top. She crossed it and found the path in the bramble hedge that led up the hill overlooking the beach. Over the other side of that hill was another path that led down to Berrydown Farm, where pints of foaming, creamy milk, freshly churned butter, thick slices of bacon and fat brown eggs would be waiting.

She climbed over carpets of thyme and eyebright, studded with yolk-yellow bee orchids, and pushed through the bracken, its sharp scent reminding her of childhood. Butterflies darted before her on the path almost as if leading the way, too quick to identify – flashes of white and red and brown and palest blue, always just out of reach.

At the top of the hill was a bench, and she stopped for a rest, closing her eyes. She breathed in and tried to count all the different sounds of birdsong she could hear, tuning her ear. It took concentration, but she thought she could define at least six. A chirrup, a chatter, a two-tone whistle; the coo of a wood pigeon, the keening of a gull overhead. Of all the noise, when she opened her eyes, she could only see two of the perpetrators: a stonechat fluttering across the gorse, and a stout bullfinch sitting on a branch of hawthorn.

She could see for miles across the ocean from here, around the spit of land to the left as far as the point further around the bay, not visible from the beach hut. Darker shapes lurked under the surface of the water – Harry convinced the children when they were smaller that they were the shadows of giant sharks. Elspeth told him off for scaring them but they loved believing him, or pretending to. She smiled at the memory. He was a terrible tease.

It truly was God's own country. Not that she had much faith in God any more. Somehow, when she needed him most, he had become elusive. Had she not believed enough when she was younger? Was that her punishment?

She stood up to push on, a quarter of a mile still to go. Perhaps she should have brought one of the grandchildren with her, but she didn't want to wake them. This was their holiday. Their downtime after a summer term of exams and sports days and prize-givings. They needed time to rest, unwind, grow. As far as she was concerned, they could do what they liked during the week they were with her.

She knew it might be the last time she would have all three of them here. Harry would be leaving school next summer and would probably be off on a gap year. The others might not want to come without him. They would grow out of the beach hut, and her, gradually, peeling off to do their own thing – a summer job, a stay with a friend abroad – and of course that was only right and proper.

Nothing stayed the same. Elspeth knew that. And maybe it was best to keep ahead of the game. Change things before change was forced upon her. She thought of the letter that had been slid under the door two days ago. Typed on headed paper, it was to the point.

Hello. We are writing to you in case you might consider selling your beach hut. We have a young family of three boys, and it has long been a dream of ours to have a hut on Everdene Sands so we can spend the summer by the sea – two of the boys are very keen surfers and the third is mad on bodyboarding and won't be too far behind! We have funds available and could complete very quickly. We would love and cherish it as much as you have, as we understand how important it must be

*to you. Please get in touch if you are interested. With
love from the Elphick Family.*

Underneath was a mobile number, and a photo of three
blond-haired boys in swimming trunks and wetsuits,
smiling widely.

As soon as she read it, Elspeth was tempted. Rumours
of beach hut prices abounded every summer, and the
thought of the big cash injection she would get was very
enticing. Harry had left her comfortable, but there wasn't
much room for large purchases. The house would need
maintaining. At some point she would need a new car.
And the beach hut itself was badly in need of some care
and attention: the roof felt was flapping, the steps were
rotting and needed replacing.

Perhaps it was time for someone else to have it. And
then she could put the money to better use. She could put
some of it aside for the grandchildren to use as a deposit
to buy their own house, in time. There was no way they'd
be able to get onto the property ladder otherwise. Selling
the beach hut would give them each a decent lump sum.
Somehow, that made her feel better. You had to move
with the times and your needs.

Although it would be painful. It was the beach hut
that had brought her and Harry together, after all. For
a moment, her mind wandered back to a summer day
more than fifty years ago. A group of young university

friends, carefree, the whole of their lives in front of them. It could almost be yesterday, she thought. For a moment, she wondered what had become of the others: Dickon and Octavia and Juliet. They'd lost touch. Of course they had. But that day had cemented her future with Harry.

If this was going to be her last summer here, she would cherish this week. Use the time to get to know each of them individually, and give them as much of her wisdom as she could, so they would feel they could talk to her if they needed to. Things might not stay the same, she thought, but she could try to be a constant. That was the role of a grandparent, to never change.

She headed down the hill to the farm shop. She remembered when it was a tumbledown shed that sold a few potatoes and some purple sprouting broccoli. Now it was a huge rustic barn bursting with produce: ripe soft-rind cheeses, charcuterie, baked goods. More of a delicatessen. She loved the ritual of coming here. She piled her basket high with everything they might need for the day. A crusty loaf, butter, bananas, Greek yoghurt. Eggs and bacon.

When she got back to the hut, she was astonished to find all three of them up. Not dressed – they were still in t-shirts and jogging bottoms, and Meg was in a fleecy onesie with rabbit ears – but they were all fizzing with the excitement they'd been full of when they were little. It gladdened her heart.

'We're making you breakfast,' said Meg, taking the basket off her. 'Go and sit down.'

'Oh!' said Elspeth. 'Well, that's very kind.'

She sat in her battered old armchair, settling into its familiar lumps, realising that the strenuous walk had taken more out of her than she realised. Edward brought her over a mug of dark brown tea, and she watched as the three of them bickered and teased each other, pulling out saucepans and bowls, rummaging through her purchases, using every utensil in the tiny kitchen. Harry had built it for her over forty years ago out of bits of old wood he'd kept in the garage. She'd painted it pale blue, and there were still runs on the front of the doors where the gloss had dripped, and most of the handles had fallen off. How many eggs had she boiled on that tiny stove? How many tins of soup or baked beans had she heated up? Hundreds and hundreds.

She closed her eyes as the delicious smells wafted over: there was bacon, and something sweeter, and the scent of fresh coffee too. It was warm in the sunshine and she could feel herself drifting away.

She started as she felt a hand on her shoulder and looked up to see Harry standing over her. How could he be there? Was she dreaming? But there he was, his hair copper-bright.

'Harry?'

'Yes. It's me.'

Oh, the warmth in his voice. She smiled, and a feeling of comfort crept over her. And then her eyes slid into focus and she realised it wasn't her Harry, the Harry who had shaken her hand over the tennis net all those years ago, but his namesake. Their grandson.

'Granny? Breakfast's ready.' He had the same easy smile as his grandpa. 'We thought we'd eat outside. Come on.'

He held out a hand to pull her from the depths of the chair. She covered up her disappointment and confusion, and followed him outside. There was a feast on the rickety old table, and a pile of tin plates, and her heart buckled at the sight of the effort they had gone to just for her: putting the orange juice into a jug when normally they would have poured it straight from the carton, carefully laying out the butter on a saucer rather than sticking their knives straight into the packet.

'We've made banana pancakes,' said Meg proudly, holding out a plate with a towering stack of golden pancakes surrounded by slices of banana.

'And bacon. Because a holiday's not a holiday without a bacon sandwich,' declared Edward.

'You can have both,' said Harry.

'Oh,' said Elspeth. 'How wonderful.'

And she sat in the sun as they fussed around her, the three of them, and she felt her heart fill with pride at what magnificent human beings they had become, and thought how proud her Harry would be of them for looking after her.

Later, when they had all gone off surfing, she went to find the letter. She thought she had folded it up and put it behind the bread bin. But it wasn't there. She searched high and low, but it was nowhere to be seen. She felt panicky. Was this the first sign of some kind of dementia? She lived in dread of losing her marbles. She'd definitely kept it. She knew she had.

And now she had no way of getting in contact with whoever had sent it. She tried to remember their family name, but it escaped her. And she certainly couldn't remember the number. Perhaps they had put the letter through all the beach hut doors on Everdene? She could ask her neighbours if they had a copy?

Maybe she had thrown it away? She opened the cupboard door under the sink and pulled out the uselessly small bin. She emptied the contents carefully, rooting through coffee grounds and egg shells. At the bottom she found it, torn into tiny pieces, soaked with bin goo. Unreadable.

She turned to see Harry standing in the doorway. There was a look of guilt on his face.

'It was all of us,' he said. 'Meg found it, while you were out. We were worried you would sell. But we don't ever want to lose this place.' He looked anguished – a mixture of shame and anxiety. 'We were going to see if we could afford to buy it between us. We've all got money saved up – birthday money, and Edward won a premium bond, and we thought Dad might lend us the rest.'

Meg appeared in the doorway behind him and her cheeks went red. 'It was me that tore it up. I can't bear the thought of anyone else in here.'

Elspeth was flooded with relief, overjoyed that they were so adamant. Now she had the perfect reason not to make a difficult decision.

'Darlings, as long as you want to come here, I will never sell. I just thought perhaps you'd grown out of it, and it was a bore coming here, and you'd rather be off somewhere else.'

'No way!' said Edward, bringing up the rear. 'We don't ever want to go anywhere else on holiday. It's perfect here. It's where we belong.'

'In that case,' said Elspeth, 'the bin's the right place for it.'

She stuffed all the rubbish back in the bin with a smile.

She would make the hut over to the three of them instead. If one day in the future they decided they wanted to sell it, for whatever reason, they could sort it out between them. Happy, carefree days by the sea were far more important than a deposit on a house.

'It's a cheek,' said Meg. 'Sending a letter like that. Who do they think they are?'

'But who wouldn't want this place? You can't blame them,' said Edward.

'Well, they've got a bloody long wait. We'll never sell. Never.' Harry was as determined as his grandfather, and Elspeth smiled to herself.

'There's a lot that needs doing, though,' said Elspeth. 'The roof's coming off. The floorboards are rotten. And without Grandpa—'

'We'll fix it,' said Harry. 'Write a list, and we'll do it this week. Me and Edward can get the bus to the DIY shop.'

'And me,' said Meg. 'I'm handy with a hammer. We do DIY at school.'

So they sat in the sunshine, eating the last of the banana pancakes, writing out all the things that needed to be done, and a shopping list, and Elspeth was astonished at how enthusiastic they were about the project. She hoped their enthusiasm would last, for the hut would be theirs by the time she had got back home and talked to her solicitor. She thought it probably would. They were certainly engrossed in their plans.

'A beach hut is for life,' said Meg, summing it up for all of them. And as Elspeth looked down the row of huts, smiling at the memory of the first time she had come here, and how it had felt like home the moment she set eyes on it, she felt certain that Harry would agree.

'A beach hut is for life,' she murmured, and tucked into the last pancake which they had all decided should be hers.

BREAKFAST RECIPES

❋

*T*here is nothing more exhilarating or life-affirming than waking up at the seaside, watching the sun peep over the horizon, gradually spreading a gilded light over the water, changing the colours from pearl-grey to a bright blue as the salty air kisses your skin.

Not everyone in my house shares my enthusiasm for watching the sun come up, and I'm secretly rather glad. I love nothing better than getting up before everyone else and padding around, making coffee and deciding what to have for breakfast. There is a certain pleasure in being the only one up yet feeling the presence of your loved ones as they slumber then gradually emerge, one by one, in need of rehydration and caffeine and sustenance.

Now is the time for an early morning dog walk or swim. I can be sure that if I don't fit in the exercise first thing it will never happen … Usually for me it's a dog walk with my miniature schnauzer Zelda, together with my friend Alice and her wire-haired dachshunds Gimli and Delphi. An hour's brisk trot across the damp sand and we put the world to rights.

Sometimes I go and join in a beach yoga session – downward dog in the sand is definitely a challenge, usually leaving me weak with laughter. A dip in the sea is exhilarating and bracing: every time I have to steel myself to take the plunge but afterwards I feel a million dollars.

Then it's back home to lure everyone out of bed. I often buy bags of croissants and pains au chocolat to leave on the side for everyone to help themselves. And nothing says the weekend or holiday time like fried bacon or sausages squashed between slices of white bread and squirted with ketchup, but you don't need a recipe for that.

I also love a 'breakfast board', reminiscent of the very best hotel offerings. A big plate with some Parma ham and chunks of Emmental or Manchego; a tumble of fruit (melon and grapes and pineapple; some fresh peaches or nectarines); bowls of creamy Greek yoghurt; fresh bread and pastries; local honey and homemade jam. It's a lovely lazy start to the day and it can sit there until everyone has had their fill.

But if there's time, I love to set everyone up for the day with one of these favourites: a little extra effort goes a long way first thing in the morning.

Banana pancakes

These are inspired by the iconic beach song by Jack Johnson.
You can't listen to it without a smile on your face, and
somehow the making of banana pancakes is the ultimate
demonstration of love, whether they are for family, friends
or a special someone. Sit on the steps with a plateful and
watch the sea. Bliss.

SERVES 4 (ABOUT 8 PANCAKES)

180g plain flour

½ tsp baking powder

1 tbsp caster sugar

1 ripe banana, mashed until runny

1 × 250g tub ricotta – empty it then use as a measuring cup

1 tub milk

3 large eggs, separated

Butter for frying

To serve

2 bananas, sliced

Maple syrup

(Play Jack Johnson loud while cooking.)

Combine the dry ingredients in one bowl. Mix together the mashed banana, ricotta, milk and egg yolks in another bowl. Whisk the egg whites until they form stiff peaks.

Stir the ricotta mix into the dry ingredients, then fold in the egg whites.

Melt the butter in a standard-size non-stick frying pan over a medium-low heat. Using the empty ricotta tub, pour just under half a tub of the batter at a time into the melted butter. Cook for 2–3 minutes on one side until you can see tiny bubbles over the surface, then flip and cook for another 2 minutes. You can cook two to three pancakes at a time, adding a little extra butter to the pan each time, but keep a sharp eye on the heat to make sure they don't catch.

Wrap the cooked pancakes in foil and keep warm in a low oven. When you have a lovely pile, drizzle with maple syrup and surround with the banana slices.

Shakshuka

The smell of these Middle Eastern eggs cooking on the stove top is guaranteed to lure your guests from beneath their duvet. The chilli gets your endorphins going, and the smoky tomato mixture cuts into the richness of the egg. I cook this in a flat-bottomed wok, but you can use a frying pan.

SERVES 2

½ tbsp coconut oil (or olive oil if you prefer)

I red onion, finely chopped

I red chilli, finely chopped

½ red or yellow pepper, or mixture of both for colour, thinly sliced

2 garlic cloves, finely chopped

½ tsp smoked paprika

½ tsp ground cumin

Sea salt to taste

I × 400g tin chopped tomatoes

I tsp dark soft brown sugar, or to taste

4 eggs

Handful of chopped fresh coriander or flat-leaf parsley

Melt the coconut oil in a lidded wok or frying pan over a medium heat, add the onion and sweat for 2 minutes. Add the chilli, pepper slices and garlic. Cook gently for 5 minutes until everything is nice and soft. Sprinkle in the spices and sea salt and add the tomatoes along with a quarter-tin of water to stop the mixture getting too thick. Add the sugar – I put in a teaspoon just to give it a little sweetness. Turn down the heat, cover and cook for about 15 minutes until all the flavours are mingled and dense. If it looks a bit too thick and dry add a little more water.

Make four indentations in the sauce, crack an egg into each one and cook over a low heat. It will take about 10 minutes for them to whiten – you might need to tilt the pan a little to distribute the whites and get them to cook evenly. Keep an eye on the yolks and, depending on whether you prefer them runny or firm, take off the heat when they're done to your liking. Scatter over your herb of choice and serve.

Garlic mushrooms

When I was a student in Bristol, my Saturday treat was to
go to Daphne's Café in Montpelier and have mushrooms on
toast. Rich, flavoursome and luxurious, mushrooms benefit
from long, slow cooking in butter, but you have to be patient.
It's well worth it!

This dish also makes a great starter for an evening meal.

SERVES 4

8 large field or portobello mushrooms
100g butter
2 garlic cloves, finely chopped
1 fresh chilli, thinly sliced, or a pinch of chilli flakes (optional)
Large bunch flat-leaf parsley, finely chopped
Sliced sourdough, toasted, or crusty bread, to serve

Cut the mushrooms in half, then thinly slice each semi-circle.
Melt the butter in a wok or frying pan over a medium heat,
then add the garlic and chilli, if using. Soften the garlic slightly,
making sure it doesn't burn, then add the mushrooms and
stir until thoroughly coated in the garlicky butter (add more
butter, or a glug of olive oil, if the mixture seems a little dry).
Turn down the heat and let the mushrooms melt into buttery

blackness until they are super-soft – up to 30 minutes, but keep an eye on them. Finish with handfuls of the chopped parsley. Serve either on toasted sourdough, or with crusty bread to mop up the juices.

Bacon and spinach frittata muffins

These are basically portable bacon and eggs, and can be made in advance. You can change the filling to suit your own taste – snips of pepper, feta, mushrooms, sweetcorn, chunks of sausage or chorizo. They can be reheated in the oven or in the microwave but are perfectly nice cold. If eating hot from the oven, roast some cherry tomatoes to serve on the side.

MAKES 6 LARGE MUFFINS

200g cherry tomatoes on the vine,
snipped into small bunches

Olive oil

200g lardons – smoked or unsmoked, whichever you prefer

200g fresh baby leaf spinach

6 large eggs

Sea salt and freshly ground black pepper

100g grated Cheddar cheese

Preheat the oven to 200°C/fan 180°C/gas mark 6.

Pop the cherry tomatoes in a roasting tin, drizzle with olive oil and put in the oven to slow-roast, about 20 minutes.

Meanwhile, fry the lardons until cooked through and getting crispy. Put the spinach in a colander and pour over a kettle of boiling water to wilt. Squeeze dry then roughly chop so it doesn't clump. Whisk the eggs thoroughly in a mixing bowl then season.

Grease a 6-hole muffin tin or pop a muffin case in each hole (these make the muffins more portable). Divide the spinach, lardons and cheese evenly between the muffin holes and pour over the egg. Put in the oven, alongside the tomatoes, for about 18 minutes – make sure they are cooked through but not dry.

Serve with the clusters of roasted tomatoes if eating straight away, or set aside to cool before storing for later use.

Guacamole and soft-boiled egg on rye sourdough

I could eat guacamole at any time of the day or night. My youngest son has proclaimed it as the food he could live on for the rest of his life if he could only choose one thing. The only snag, of course, is the avocado conundrum – how to catch them when they are perfect? Nothing makes my heart sink faster than opening an avocado and seeing blackened flesh. And quite often the avocados sold as 'ripe and ready' are like bullets. As I eat so many, I have overcome this by making sure I buy a couple every time I go to the supermarket. I check them daily, then use them just as they are starting to give.

Handy tip: to skin your tomato, score a cross into the skin, cover with boiling water and leave for 10 minutes. The skin will then peel off easily.

SERVES 2

2 large eggs

1 large avocado

1 large beef tomato, skinned and finely diced

2 spring onions, thinly sliced

Pinch of chilli flakes

Zest and juice of 1 lime
Sea salt
4 slices rye sourdough, toasted
1 radish, sliced super-thin
A few chives, finely chopped

Have a bowl of iced water ready. Bring a pan of water to the boil, then add the eggs. Boil for 6 minutes – don't forget to set a timer as the timing is crucial if you want soft centres!

While the eggs are boiling, mash the avocado. You might like your avocado chunky or you might prefer it baby-food smooth – it's up to you. Add the tomato and spring onions, mixing thoroughly. Then add the chilli flakes, lime juice and zest and salt to taste.

After the 6 minutes, remove the eggs from the boiling water, plunge them immediately into the iced water and leave for 3 minutes. This will stop the cooking process and help you remove the shells.

Pile the avocado onto the toasted rye bread. Peel the eggs carefully, cut in half with a very sharp knife and perch on top of the avocado, then serve with the radish slices and chives.

Try adding some sriracha sauce if you have some – it goes well with this dish and adds an extra kick.

Tropical overnight oats

I first discovered overnight oats in the form of Bircher muesli when I was upgraded to business class (for the first and only time in my life!) on a flight. That version was drenched in double cream and almost stopped my heart on the spot, but there was something about the texture that I loved. This version is somewhat healthier and quite zingy. There's something satisfying about overnight soaking – it makes me feel organised and efficient to wake up to a bowl of oats ready to be zhuzhed up. For the mango, I use the tubs of freshly prepared chunks readily available from supermarkets, as whole mango can be as tricky as avocado on the ripeness front and I've never quite mastered the art of cutting them up.

SERVES 2

150g porridge oats

375ml semi-skimmed milk, or dairy-free milk of your choice

1 lime

1 × 280g tub fresh mango chunks, cut into small pieces

Runny honey

Dairy-free coconut yoghurt or Greek yoghurt

Toasted pumpkin seeds

The night before, mix the oats in the milk and leave in the fridge to soak. In a separate bowl, zest the lime over the mango chunks and squeeze over the juice. Then go to bed safe in the knowledge you will have a lovely breakfast waiting the next day.

In the morning, divide the oats between two bowls and top with the mango.

Finish with a drizzle of honey, a dollop of your chosen yoghurt and a sprinkling of toasted pumpkin seeds.

Pimped porridge

If it's chilly or wet, or if you are at the beach in autumn, when the sun is lower in the sky and the air is sharp and fringed with mist, there is nothing more satisfying than a bowl of porridge. Porridge gets a bad rap because it is often cooked without love and care or attention and you end up with a bowl of gloopy wallpaper paste. But a sharp eye and a few thoughtful additions can turn it into a bowl of luxury that is warming and filling. Buy good oats and cook them well and you will get a heavenly creamy carrier for all sorts of flavours that is like being wrapped in a blanket. I always keep a tin of Flahavan's oats for porridge or flapjacks on my shelf (true to my Irish roots!). Porridge is divine served with cream and a carapace of soft brown sugar, but this is my favourite 'pimped' version.

SERVES 2

250ml full-fat milk

250ml water

100g good-quality porridge oats

1 tbsp light soft brown sugar

1 tsp ground ginger

Zest and juice of 1 orange

6 Medjool dates, chopped

Put the milk and water in a saucepan, add the oats and sugar and stir thoroughly, then bring to the boil. Lower the heat and cook for 5 minutes, watching like a hawk to make sure the porridge doesn't catch on the bottom of the pan. Stir in the ginger, orange zest and juice and half of the chopped dates and cook for a further 5 minutes. Take off the heat and leave to cool a little. Spoon into bowls and top with the remaining dates. The addition of cream, Greek yoghurt or extra sugar is entirely up to you!

AN EARLY MORNING SWIM

I'm in the throes of endeavouring to become a year-round swimmer, inspired by a friend whose Instagram account documents her daily swim with friends on the Dorset coast come rain, shine, fog, mist, hail, snow, ice … I yearn for an ounce of her intrepid bravery. As I write this, the sea is starting to cool rapidly after the warmth of summer, and getting in without donning a wetsuit becomes more of an ordeal. But a group of us have sworn to keep going for as long as we can. Maybe we will even make it in on Christmas Day? We're spurred on by the evidence that cold-water swimming has a positive effect on mental and physical health, and it's good to have a challenge. Character-building.

I phone my neighbouring friend early in the morning. Fancy a swim? She laughs nervously before agreeing. We've dared each other now. We have a pact. We pack up our togs and our towels and meet to walk halfway down the beach where we are unlikely to be seen by anyone else. This is a private moment! (We do, when we walk our dogs, see a man who swims *au naturel* each day without any self-consciousness, but we don't have his bravado.)

There's a point at which we can tell each other this is a silly idea and go for a coffee instead. But we don't. We tentatively put our beach bags down, eyeing the frill of waves on the shore. How cold will it be? We walk to the edge, silent with both excitement and dread but united in our daring.

We stride into the sea, gasping as the liquid wraps itself around our ankles, splashing ourselves to acclimatise. But strangely, after a moment or two, it's no longer a shock, and we persevere, walking through the shallows. As we reach knee height we are slowed down by the weight of the water, but we plough on, getting used to the cold. As the water comes up to our thighs, we know we have to brace ourselves. By the time it reaches our waists, we can barely breathe, but there is no turning back. This is the point we have to quite literally take the plunge and dive under. The waves are getting higher and are taunting us, sometimes flicking us with icy droplets that make us squeal. We look at each other ... one ... two ... three ...

I plunge beneath the next wave. The world changes in an instant. It's blue and slow and dreamlike and silent. I feel a burst of triumph that I had the courage to do this. It's wonderful.

We pop up and look at each other, grinning. For the

next fifteen minutes, we play. We splash and dive and float, twisting and turning, sinuous in a way that we never are on land. I feel graceful, something I rarely feel on terra firma. My body, not inhibited by gravity, will do almost whatever I ask of it.

I lie on my back and stare at the clouds. There is just sand and sea and sky and me. I could be the only person in the world. I am weightless, boneless, both my mind and body drifting. I'm hyper-aware but also switched off. I feel safe and secure, cradled by the water. Is this what being mindful means?

I turn so I can watch the sun rising above the water. The sunrise is one of life's certainties. I reflect on how lucky I am, how everyone should be able to do this and allow their troubles to float away.

Afterwards, we peel off our wet things. I wriggle into my towelling hooded robe, my skin tingling, my mind alert, my heart still pounding from the adrenaline. We congratulate each other on our fortitude. We scurry back up the beach, jubilant, safe in the knowledge we have earned our cappuccino and ready to face whatever the day brings us. Nothing will be as challenging as braving that water!

Picnic food

I've Seen
That Face Before

Anna would never have believed she could be happy again. Three years ago, she was on the verge of a nervous breakdown. Strung out, exhausted, miserable, stressed. Eaten up by the injustice of life, when all she had ever done for her staff was try to be supportive. But there was always one, wasn't there? Someone who saw the world entirely differently from you and chose to misunderstand your motives, twisting them to their own advantage. And in the end, Anna couldn't take it any longer. Her resignation would be seen as an admission of guilt, but she knew she was innocent and that was all that really mattered.

The company had feigned protest when she handed in her letter, but she knew she was tainted. No one liked a tribunal. No one liked accusations of bullying and constructive dismissal. She was guilty of neither, but people still looked at her doubtfully. It rocked her confidence. It took all the joy out of what she did. Before the court case, she had been rising high and was regularly approached by other companies. Afterwards, even though she had won, she knew she would be stuck where she was, with no chance of promotion or being headhunted.

She was immediately put on gardening leave. She had no idea what she wanted to do, but she knew the corporate life was no longer for her. She wanted a complete change, to forget the whole sorry business. So she'd signed up to do a patisserie course at her local college. She went from being someone who lived on Marks and Spencer ready meals to banging out brioches and rum babas with ease. Being a stickler for detail and precise about timings, she was, it turned out, a natural baker.

And now, here she was, the owner of The Beach Bun, a seaside bakery in a little row of shops in Everdene. The premises had been a rather gloomy and old-fashioned sweet shop that sold homemade fudge and rock. She had taken on the lease for five years, put in a new kitchen, painted everything white and got a carpenter to put up chunky oak shelves with iron brackets. And from there she sold all her favourite baked goods. There was a zinc counter with half a dozen high stools where people could have a coffee and their pastry of choice.

It was exhausting. Even more exhausting than her old job. She got up at five every morning and made sure she was in bed by ten at night, otherwise she couldn't have managed. She took on several other members of staff to help. But she loved it. She wouldn't swap it for the world.

Once, she would have been out of the house by seven, dressed in her suit and high heels, laptop ready to be whipped out on the train until she reached work. Now first thing in the morning she did the croissant run along the row of huts on the beach. She had a big wicker basket filled with pastries: pains au chocolat, pains au raisin, pecan swirls, cinnamon buns, blueberry muffins. Her offerings were one up from anything you could get in the supermarket: her pastry was flakier, her filling plumper, her icing thicker. It was a good way to start the day; people were always happy to see her.

Then she went back to open the shop. On went the Italian coffee machine, pumping its rich scent out into the street. The shelves behind the counter were piled high with bread and rolls and focaccia. The counter was filled with savoury tarts and spanakopita and Spanish tortilla, sausage rolls and Scotch eggs, and, of course, plump, bulging pasties. Everything you could possibly fancy for a picnic on the beach.

From nine o'clock there was a steady stream of customers until she closed at three. She had to shut then because she'd never get the next day's bake done otherwise.

This year, she was going to be in profit. Her investment and hard work were going to start paying off. And she couldn't have been happier. The HR manager she had once been seemed like another person. She certainly looked different, with her once-bobbed hair well past her shoulders and bleached by the sun, and her baggy linen dungarees with a Breton shirt underneath. Her myriad work suits had gone off to a charity that provided interview clothes for women who couldn't afford a smart outfit. She hoped they had brought luck to whoever wore them.

There had only been one blip in the past three years, and she should have seen that coming. Of course, men like Dino didn't stick around for women like her. Men like Dino had wanderlust; and another kind of lust too. He was beguiling, infuriating, magnetic.

And sitting on the third stool along when she got back to the bakery this morning.

He was sipping an espresso and chewing on an apricot Danish, as if he hadn't announced out of the blue at the end of last summer that he was off to Santa Fe for the winter. He'd developed his own brand of aqua yoga and was in high demand with celebrity clients. If his body was anything to go by, his regime certainly worked. With his blond mane, sea-green eyes and his bronzed limbs, he was his own best advert. He worked in Everdene every summer for a reclusive actress who had a house overlooking the beach. Three hours a day training and the rest of the time was his. Last summer, he'd spent most of that time with Anna. Until his vanishing act. She hadn't seen or heard from him since. Yet here he was, as if he'd never been away.

Anna had every intention of walking straight past him and hiding in the kitchen until he had gone. But he put out his hand and grabbed her wrist. Pulled her to him and lifted her hand to his mouth, kissing the back of her fingers.

'Babe.'

She wasn't falling for it. He was an arrogant, thoughtless … well, not quite monster, because he had many redeeming qualities. But he was selfish. A selfish pig.

A selfish pig who was making her tummy flip over and over and unseemly thoughts enter her mind.

'Dino,' she said. 'Fancy seeing you here.'

'I gather the pastries are out of this world.' His eyes danced with mischief.

'They certainly are.'

'And the owner.' He had on a necklace with a golden dinosaur charm. A play on his name. A gift from some doting client, no doubt. It nestled at the base of his throat. She remembered pressing her lips to the hollow in his collarbone, feeling the pulse underneath. What did the dinosaur mean? Nothing? Something? Everything? To someone. Who?

She gave him a tight smile and tried to pull away. 'Well. It's lovely to see you, but I've got work to do.'

'Anna.' The way he said her name made her insides feel like melted butter. 'Come for a swim when you've finished, eh?'

She put up her hand, shaking her head. She felt angry. Didn't he realise what he'd done to her, leaving her in

47

the lurch like that with only twenty-four hours' notice? She hadn't heard a word from him. It was only now that she was starting to feel normal again. Not so bruised and battered.

'It's how I roll,' he told her the day before he left. 'I move around the world. Wherever the work takes me. Someone reaches out and I go.'

'You could have warned me.' She thought how needy she sounded as she spoke, but dammit – she deserved a bit of respect, didn't she?

She wasn't going to put herself through it again. But Dino was insistent.

'We can go for a paddle. I've got a spare board. It's perfect out there today.'

He'd taught her to stand-up paddle last summer, and she'd loved it, gliding across the water on the SUP board. She hesitated. What harm could it do? The conditions were indeed perfect. Quite calm beyond the frill of surf at the water's edge. It was one of her favourite things to do, head out towards the spit of land that went around to the next bay. Sometimes there were even dolphins.

His eyes were on her and she felt uncertain. It's just a paddle, she told herself. They certainly couldn't get up to anything untoward out there.

'I finish at three,' she said, and walked away, hating herself for giving in. But feeling more alive than she had since he left.

'Dino's out there,' her assistant baker Steph said, fixing her with a stern eye as she came into the kitchen. There were racks of cooling tarts and quiches, ready for the lunchtime rush. Steph was mixing up spinach with feta, grating in lemon rind.

'Yep,' said Anna, pulling out a mixing bowl and placing it on the table, looking up at the whiteboard to see what needed preparing next.

'Tell me you're not seeing him.' Steph had seen how much of a wreck Anna was when Dino left.

'We're just going for a paddle.'

'Anna.' Steph's tone was stern. 'Don't do it. He nearly destroyed you.'

'He didn't, though. I'm here, aren't I?' Anna poured a cloud of flour into the bowl.

'I thought more of you,' said Steph, shaking her head. 'I thought you had more self-respect.'

She started layering up sheets of filo pastry, basting each one with melted butter.

Anna sighed. It was the chemistry that was the problem. That inexplicably powerful equation that drew her and Dino together. The formula was impossible to resist. It was the same chemistry that happened when you combined certain ingredients: flour, sugar, fat. The result was irresistible. She tried to explain this to Steph, who rolled her eyes and picked up a plump, sugary Chelsea bun that had just come out of the oven.

'If I told you that if you ate this, it would make you violently ill, would you eat it anyway, just for the pleasure? And then spend the next few days with stomach cramp, being sick into the toilet? Dino is poison!'

'Okay, okay.' Anna knew her friend spoke the truth. Dino *was* poison. She *would* get hurt. Even if he was utterly delicious and she longed to devour him. 'I hear you, Steph. I won't go.'

She was strong enough to go back on her word. It wouldn't kill him. There would be another Anna somewhere in Everdene. Some girl willing to give Dino her undivided attention and fulfil his needs. He would show her a good time too. She shivered as she remembered how good he was at massage, those long, strong fingers caressing every sinew, making her melt into the mattress. No wonder he was in such high demand.

But emotional needs – he didn't look after those so much. What he had done had been brutal and uncaring, and he seemed to have no conscience. How else could he swan back in here and simply pick up where he left off? Someone needed to teach him that he couldn't treat people like that.

Maybe it should be her? Maybe she should be the one to teach him a lesson? No one else had stood up to him before. And if it wasn't pointed out to him that his behaviour was out of order, how was he to know?

Anna furiously rubbed butter into the flour, but she

couldn't help wondering if Dino was still in the café, or if he had left. She looked at the clock. Another five hours before they were due to meet. She had plenty to get on with in that time to take her mind off it.

Somehow the hours flew by, and, before Anna knew it, it was a quarter to three. Dino would be waiting at the slipway that led to the beach, two paddle boards leaning up against the wall. She imagined him in his board shorts, his torso, ripped and gleaming, his strong legs, his broad shoulders. His golden hair, which he'd tie up in a knot on top of his head before they went in.

She tried to steady her breathing as she tidied up her work area. She would have to come back at six to put on tomorrow's bakes. Steph looked after the small team that would keep things going between three and six while Anna had some breathing space. She slipped out of the back door while Steph was out of the kitchen. She didn't want her asking any questions.

She walked along the parade of shops, weaving her way among the holidaymakers who were on the hunt for fish and chips, buckets and spades, postcards to send home. The sun was starting its slow descent. The sea glimmered turquoise, reggae drifted out of a surf shop and once again Anna felt grateful that she'd landed on her feet by taking the risk and coming here. The flat above the bakery was only tiny, but it had two Velux windows that let in the sun, and at night she could see the stars in the sky smiling down on her. She'd painted everything white, then picked up various bits of rattan furniture, some potted plants and some brightly coloured throws to make it a bright and welcoming space to live in. She hadn't let anyone share her rather lumpy double bed since Dino. She had been too wary.

She walked down the slipway to the beach and, just as she'd imagined, there he was, waiting for her.

'I knew you'd come,' he smiled, and she smiled back. She peeled off her dungarees and shirt, revealing her costume underneath, picked up one of the SUP boards and grabbed a paddle.

'Come on, then,' she said, and they headed out across the sand. The tide was on its way in, only halfway up the beach, so it took a while to reach the water. They lay their boards flat then pushed their way through several sets of waves before reaching the calm of the back. They clambered onto their boards, standing up then using the paddles to push themselves further out to sea.

Anna never felt more at peace than when she was out on the water like this. Bright blue as far as she could see, with the sky meeting the ocean. A gentle wind helped them drift along. Birds soared overhead, even freer than they were. She watched Dino, slightly ahead of her, watched the muscles on his arms contract as he paddled. She thought of his smooth skin on hers, his hair tickling her cheek, his strong fingers stroking the small of her back. The memories were as crystal clear as the water beneath them.

They glided to a halt, stopping for a moment. The sun shimmered on the water's surface, dazzling them.

'Here we are, just you and me,' said Dino.

'Here we are.' She nodded. She could see the dinosaur glinting. She could just imagine the kind of woman who'd given it to him. Someone who thought that by giving him the gift of gold, she would somehow have a hold on him.

'I missed you,' he said.

Anna leaned on her paddle and stared at him. 'No, you didn't.'

He looked puzzled. 'What?'

'You didn't miss me. I don't suppose I entered your head until you walked back into Everdene and thought, *Oh yeah – the bakery girl was cute. Let's give her another go.*'

'Anna!' He looked wounded.

She pointed at him, her rage rising. 'You think you can walk in and out of people's lives without giving them a second thought. That they will be there for your convenience. And some of them will be dumb enough to drop everything for you, because you're golden, Dino. Just like that charm around your neck. But your gold isn't even skin deep. Underneath you're hard and cold and selfish. You're a narcissist. You use people.'

'Where is this coming from, Anna?'

'You need to know the truth. Because we all deserve

better. All the women who've fallen for your good looks, your silver tongue, your magic fingers.'

'Is this Steph's influence? I know she doesn't like me—'

'No, Dino. It's me finally figuring out the truth. For myself. There was a moment back there when I could have fallen for you again. But then I remembered how I felt when you left last year. I was devastated. I couldn't eat or sleep. I thought it was me. I wondered what I had done to deserve being abandoned. I didn't realise that I'd simply served a purpose for the summer. You're not doing it to me again.'

'I just thought … clean break!' he protested. 'I hate scenes.'

'Well, here's a scene. You're a jerk, Dino.' She threw her paddle at him and was rewarded by the sight of him losing his balance as he desperately tried to catch it. As he fell backwards into the sea, she dived neatly off her own board. He could figure out how to get both of his boards back to land.

She powered through the water with the strong crawl she had perfected over the past year. She could feel the cool sea part for her as she made for the shore, keeping her breathing even. The further she swam away from Dino, the stronger she felt. She had survived the court case, she had reinvented herself, she had built up a business that was thriving and beloved and gave other people much-needed work. She was not going to let Dino try to destroy what she had achieved. She wasn't going to be dazzled by him and fall back into his arms. And she wasn't going to let him do it to anyone else. She would make sure every girl in Everdene knew how he operated.

She reached the shallows and stood up, striding towards the shore like Ursula Andress in *Dr No*. She didn't look back to see if Dino was struggling. She walked straight on up the beach, laughing.

She was a warrior. She was a survivor. She was a total goddess!

PICNIC RECIPES

*I*t was my Irish grandmother who instilled in me my love of picnics. She was the mistress of swooping on everything that was left over in the kitchen and turning it into transportable food, piled into tin foil and Tupperware and then into her shopping basket to be put in the boot of my grandfather's Rover. We would drive along the winding lanes of Kerry, fuchsia hedges slapping at the sides, watching the round compass on his dashboard swivelling around north, south, east, west until we reached a windy, salt-drenched beach, breathed in the Atlantic and tried to see America. Flasks of soup bulked out with yesterday's rice, endless boiled eggs, cold sausages, slices of crumbly soda bread thick with butter piled high with roast chicken, date slices, Rice Krispie cakes – you never knew what you might get, but it always tasted delicious in the Irish air, and what we didn't eat her brace of Jack Russells would eagerly devour.

My picnic love endures, and I light upon any recipe that is easily portable and shareable. Cold chicken, sausages and hard-boiled eggs still remain my standard portable fare, but these are my favourite picnic staples.

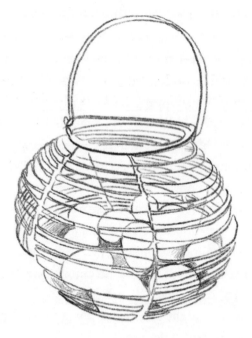

Pan bagnat

This traditional French picnic loaf is fantastic as you can customise it to suit your own tastes. The original is based on a salad Niçoise, bulging with eggs and anchovy, but there are loads of alternatives. You can lug it along in the bottom of your basket and produce it as soon as hunger begins to strike. I go for an Italian combination of flavours and textures, but there is no limit.

You can make individual versions of this with small crusty cobs if you want to do a separate pan bagnat for each person, but as picnics are about sharing and the unveiling is rather ceremonial, I stick to a whole one. Most supermarkets these days have a version of the classic French boule.

SERVES 4

1 French boule or cob or round bloomer

2 tbsp olive oil

1 tbsp pesto

4 roasted red peppers from a jar, drained and cut into strips

2 mozzarella balls, drained and thinly sliced

1 packet fresh basil leaves

2 large vine-ripened tomatoes, thinly sliced

Sea salt

6 slices Parma ham

Cut the top off the loaf about an eighth of the way down
– a little lower than if you were cutting a lid for a pumpkin.
Put the lid to one side, then scoop the bread from the centre
of the loaf until you have a crusty shell about 1cm thick.
Save the bread to make breadcrumbs – you could use them
for the Parmesan Chicken further on! Baste the inside with
the olive oil using a pastry brush, then spread pesto over
the bottom.

Now begin a layering process and fill the inside with the
rest of your ingredients – you may have to cut some of
the slices into smaller pieces to make them fit neatly.
Salt the tomatoes well as you lay them in. Repeat the layers
until you have reached the top of the loaf.

For a more authentic version, layer up tomato, slices of
egg, tuna, olives and anchovy. Or mix it up with a variety
of chargrilled vegetables from a jar (aubergine, courgette,
mushrooms), your favourite cheese (Brie or Camembert
would work well) and cured meats – chorizo, salami, bresaola
… Maybe add some crisp green cos lettuce and some
cucumber sliced lengthways.

Once you've finished your layering, pop the lid back on,
pushing it down hard to make sure it forms a seal, then wrap
the whole loaf very tightly in cling film – this helps stop the
juices from escaping during the pressing phase. Then wrap in
tin foil. Sandwich between two wooden chopping boards and

place something heavy on top. Leave for a few hours
or overnight for it all to compress and for the flavours
to develop.

Take one of the chopping boards to the beach with a very
sharp bread knife to slice it up.

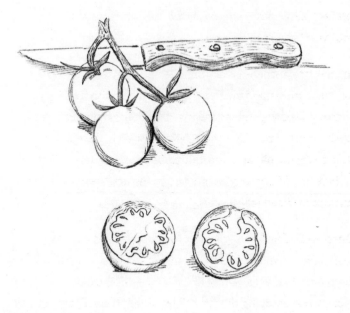

Spanakopita

This Greek pie is heavenly! Succulent spinach, salty cheese and crispy filo all combine to make the perfect lunch dish, filling but not too sleep-inducing, and it is as gorgeous cold as it is warm. Use the best feta cheese you can find, and not that slightly plastic 'salad' cheese. You want crumbly, tangy and salty.

This makes a mammoth version that serves up to ten people, with some left over for later.

SERVES 8–10

2 tbsp olive oil

100g butter

2kg fresh baby leaf spinach

2 bunches spring onions, finely chopped

2 × 250g tubs ricotta

Sea salt to taste

Zest of 1 large lemon

2 tbsp chopped fresh dill

4 eggs

2 × 200g blocks feta cheese

1 × 250g packet filo pastry

1 tbsp poppy seeds

Preheat the oven to 220°C/fan 200°C/gas mark 7.

Melt the olive oil and butter together and pour into a small bowl. You will be using this later to baste the filo and grease your baking dish.

Put the spinach in a colander and pour over boiling water to wilt – you will need to do this in batches unless you have a colander the size of a baby's bath! I then split the ingredients and do the next stage in two bowls as it's more manageable. Put half the spinach, the spring onions, a tub of ricotta and sea salt to taste into a large bowl and mix together roughly by hand, massaging the leaves as you go. Add half the lemon zest and dill and 2 eggs and mix everything together thoroughly, then crumble in a block of feta.

Repeat with the remaining ingredients in another bowl.

Use a pastry brush to grease the bottom of a large, 36×27cm, enamel or ovenproof dish with the oil and butter mixture. Line the bottom with four sheets of filo, folding them up the sides where necessary and basting each sheet as you go. Then fold a sheet of pastry lengthways over each of the long sides of the dish so that half is lining the dish and the other half is hanging over the edge. Do the same at the short ends of the dish using the short side of the pastry. (The overhanging pastry will be folded back over once the filling is in place.) Brush these four sheets with the butter and oil.

Then spoon in the spinach mixture and smooth it out evenly. Fold the four overhanging sheets over the mixture so it's nicely tucked in. Layer the remaining filo sheets over the top, covering any gaps and basting.

Take a very sharp knife and cut the top layers of filo into diamonds – it is easier to cut the pastry when raw and this will help when you come to slice it to serve. It is fiddly so make sure your knife really is sharp! Sprinkle the top with poppy seeds. Put in the oven and cook for 1 hour until the top is beautifully crisp and golden.

Pissaladière

I'm not sure how authentic this is, but it's my take on the Provençal classic. With meltingly sweet onions, uber-salty anchovies and punchy black olives, it looks stunning with its criss-cross lattice on top of the tomato.

SERVES 4

1 tbsp olive oil
3 large onions, very thinly sliced
4 large vine-ripened tomatoes, finely chopped
1 × 320g ready-rolled sheet flaky or puff pastry
100g anchovies – 2 tins or from a tub at the deli counter
70g black olives

Preheat the oven to 220°C/fan 200°C/gas mark 7.

Heat the oil in a frying pan over a medium-low heat and slide in the onions, cooking them down for a good 20–30 minutes until they are sweetly golden. Stir regularly – you don't want them to brown or burn or dry out. Once the onions have softened, add the tomatoes and cook until the tomato moisture has evaporated – about 10–15 minutes. Put the mixture in a sieve to drain off the majority of the oil and any excess liquid.

Sandwich the pastry between two baking sheets lined with parchment paper to keep it flat and to prevent sticking. Bake the pastry blind for 10 minutes, then remove from the oven. Spoon the onion mixture over the top, leaving a bit of an edge. Then lay the anchovies nose to tail in a criss-cross lattice on top of the onions. Pop an olive in the centre of each diamond. Slide back into the oven and cook for another 15 minutes.

Remove from the oven and cut into squares. It's delicious eaten warm from the oven but is also wonderful cold if you are taking it to the beach.

Parmesan chicken

The buttermilk makes this chicken melt in the mouth while the outside is satisfyingly crunchy. I have never known any to be left over.

SERVES 4

8 skinless, boneless chicken thighs

2 large garlic cloves, finely chopped

Zest of 1 lemon

Rosemary sprig,
leaves removed and finely chopped

300ml buttermilk

100g panko breadcrumbs
(or whizz up some old bread)

100g grated Parmesan cheese

Sea salt and freshly ground black pepper

Cut the chicken thighs in half so you have nice chunky pieces. Stir the garlic, lemon and rosemary into the buttermilk then add the chicken. Leave for at least 2 hours, or preferably overnight.

Preheat the oven to 220°C/fan 200°C/gas mark 7.

Mix the breadcrumbs and Parmesan together. Remove the chicken pieces from the buttermilk marinade and dip them in the crumb mix, rolling them around to coat thoroughly.

Place on a greased baking tray and cook in the oven for 25 minutes. Keep an eye as you don't want the chicken pieces to dry out – test one of the pieces by cutting into it, making sure it's cooked through. If still pink, put back in the oven for 10 minutes.

Eat straight away, or cool and transport to the beach wrapped in greaseproof paper to enjoy with your picnic.

Coronation chicken

One of the nicest, plainest things to eat outdoors is a cold roast chicken, perfectly cooked so it isn't dry, eaten with brown bread and cold butter and a sprinkling of sea salt. There is something old-fashioned in its simplicity. You could have a little sharp rocket or watercress and perhaps some ripe juicy tomatoes on the side.

(To roast the perfect chicken, spread softened butter under the skin then add a sprinkling of sea salt and the zest of a lemon over the skin. Chop the lemon in half and stuff it inside the cavity. Cook at 190°C/fan 170°C/gas mark 5 for 1 hour, then remove and pierce a leg to see if the juice is running clear. If not, return to the oven for another 20 minutes. Leave to rest.)

The picnic queen, however, is Coronation Chicken, rolled out at royal celebrations since its invention for the Queen's coronation in 1953. The original version devised by Rosemary Hume includes curry powder, chopped apricots and whipped cream and was a work of inspired genius. It has been trotted out over the decades in various guises and lugged to Henley, Glyndebourne and Ascot, doled out at street parties and jubilee celebrations and, although it might seem a groaning cliché, it works every time.

This version is cheatingly quick, both tangy and creamy, and is super-easy to whip up on holiday if you have few facilities.

SERVES 4

1 × 1.5kg rotisserie chicken
(most large supermarkets have a hot-chicken counter)
or one you have pre-roasted yourself (see above)

250ml mayonnaise

250ml Greek yoghurt

300g mango chutney

Zest and juice of 1 lime

Sea salt and freshly ground black pepper

1 bunch coriander, finely chopped

Cos lettuce, leaves roughly torn, to serve

Strip the chicken and tear into bite-size pieces. Mix together the mayonnaise, yoghurt, chutney and lime zest and juice. Stir the chicken pieces through the mixture until well coated and season to taste. Sprinkle over the coriander and serve on a bed of crisp light green cos lettuce leaves.

Tortilla

Otherwise known as Spanish omelette, a tortilla is a very handy picnic item, sliced into wedges, equally delicious hot or cold, and you can sling anything that takes your fancy into the egg mixture. This is a useful dish for vegetarians, and if you want to include potato it makes a good filler.

The traditional method is to cook the tortilla in a frying pan and then flip it over to cook the other side, but this takes a little nerve and it can all fall apart or, worse, stick to the bottom. So I prefer to start the cooking on the hob and then transfer the pan (make sure it's ovenproof) to the oven to cook through and brown slightly on the top.

This recipe is for asparagus tortilla, which is light, bright and nutty in flavour.

SERVES 4 (WITH PLENTY LEFT OVER FOR LATER)

200g asparagus tips

1 tbsp butter

1 tbsp olive oil

8 eggs, beaten

Sea salt and freshly ground black pepper

Preheat the oven to 200°C/fan 180°C/gas mark 6.

Bring a pan of water to the boil and blanch the asparagus tips for 2 minutes, then drain and plunge into cold water. Melt the butter in a 20cm frying pan that can go in the oven, then add the oil. Season the eggs with salt and pepper and pour them into the pan, then add the asparagus tips, distributing them evenly. Cook over a low heat for 10 minutes until the egg mixture has started to solidify nicely, making sure the tortilla doesn't catch too much on the bottom. Pop into the oven for another 5 minutes to brown.

There is no limit to what you can add: below are a few suggestions. Some ingredients just require blanching; others need to be softened in the butter/olive oil mixture before adding the eggs.

- Spring onions, peppers, cherry tomatoes and feta cheese: soften the onions and peppers, add cherry tomatoes, then sprinkle in feta last.

- Potato and red onion: slice new potatoes to the width of a pound coin, parboil for 8 minutes then soften the onion and add the potato slices before pouring in the eggs.

- Pea and spring onion: blanch the peas and soften the onions.

- Chorizo and cherry tomatoes: fry off the chorizo and soften the tomatoes in the pan.

Tomato tarte tatin

I love tomatoes, I love tarte tatin and I love my tarte tatin
tin, so this is a really quick and simple picnic treat – although
you will probably get tomato down your front at some point
while eating it! If you can get tomatoes in a variety of colours,
the tarte tatin will look amazing.

SERVES 4–6

500g mixed baby tomatoes – cherry, plum, piccolo

1 tbsp balsamic vinegar

A few thyme sprigs, leaves removed

1 tsp soft brown sugar

1 × 320g block puff pastry

Flour, for dusting

Grated Parmesan cheese (optional)

Preheat the oven to 200°C/fan 180°C/gas mark 6.

Wash and dry the tomatoes and put in a bowl with the
vinegar and thyme leaves, stirring thoroughly to coat. Then tip
them into a 23cm baking tin and sprinkle over the sugar. Roll
out the pastry on a floured surface into a circle a tad wider
than the tin. You can, if you like a cheesy finish, sprinkle some

73

grated Parmesan over the pastry at this point and run over it with the rolling pin to bed it in. Lift the pastry and place it carefully over the tomatoes, tucking the edges firmly in. Bake in the oven for 25 minutes, remove and cool slightly then invert the tarte tatin onto a plate.

AND TO ACCOMPANY ...

Here are a few salad suggestions that will go with all of the above recipes – a good mixture of flavours and textures. They all serve 4.

Roasted tomato and mozzarella orzo salad

This is a little more exotic than the bland flaccid pasta salads of my childhood – pasta bows mixed with mayonnaise and sweetcorn! The roasted tomatoes give it a real depth of flavour, and orzo is perfect if cooked with just a little bite.

I tbsp olive oil

I garlic clove, grated

300g cherry tomatoes

200g orzo

I tbsp pesto

I × 250g tub bocconcini, halved (if you can't get bocconcini then tear a large mozzarella ball into smaller pieces)

I × 175g tub chargrilled artichokes

I bunch fresh basil, leaves torn

Sea salt and freshly ground black pepper

Preheat the oven to 220°C/fan 200°C/gas mark 7.

Whisk the oil with the grated garlic and drizzle over the cherry tomatoes with a scattering of sea salt and put in the oven to roast for 20 minutes.

Bring a large pan of salted water to the boil. Pour in the orzo and cook until al dente, about 10 minutes. Drain and refresh under the cold tap, then stir through the pesto.

Remove the tomatoes when they are just beginning to char. Let them cool then tip them into the orzo, scraping out all the juices. Add the bocconcini. Cut the artichokes into smaller pieces and add to the mixture. Stir through until it is all evenly coated, then scatter over the basil and a grinding of black pepper.

Punchy crunchy slaw

Who doesn't love a slaw? While it's tempting to pick up a tub from the supermarket, the flavour and texture is so much more interesting when you make it yourself, and it's rather therapeutic to slice and dice and chop. This is colourful and vibrant and zingy and will add bite to any picnic.

½ small red cabbage

2 large carrots, peeled

2 celery sticks

1 bunch spring onions

1 red pepper, deseeded

6 radishes

1 tsp cumin seeds

2 tbsp olive oil

1 tbsp honey

3 limes

1 garlic clove, minced with ½ tsp sea salt

1 fresh chilli, minced

1 bunch fresh coriander, chopped

Sea salt, to taste

1 tbsp pumpkin seeds, lightly toasted

Finely dice and slice all the vegetables as thinly as you can. You can grate the carrot but very fine matchsticks add extra texture if you can be bothered.

Lightly toast the cumin seeds in a frying pan to release the flavour. In the bottom of the bowl you are going to serve the salad in, whisk the olive oil, honey and the zest and juice of 2 of the limes then stir in the garlic, chilli, cumin seeds and half the coriander until all the flavours are mingled. Tip in the slaw mix and toss until everything is coated in the dressing. Add sea salt to taste. Sprinkle the pumpkin seeds and the rest of the coriander over the top, then squeeze over the remaining lime.

Celeriac remoulade

Whenever we go to France, I buy tubs of celeriac remoulade and live off dollops of it with slices of Bayonne ham. I love the nutty celery flavour and the firmness and the sharp mustardy edge.

1 medium celeriac (about 600g)
100ml mayonnaise
100ml crème fraîche
1 tbsp grainy mustard
Zest and juice of 1 lemon
Sea salt and freshly ground black pepper

Cut the celeriac into wedges then peel it and coarsely grate the flesh – this is the time-consuming bit and I can never get it as uniformly beautiful as the bought tubs, but this will be more rustic! You may have a food processor that will do the job for you. Mix the mayo with the crème fraîche, mustard and lemon zest and juice then fold in the grated celeriac until evenly coated. Season to taste.

Smashed cucumbers

I'm crazy about these – crunchy, sweet but sour, fresh, super-easy yet somehow exotic and as far removed from an unimaginative side salad of slightly dried-out sliced cucumber as you can get.

2 large cucumbers

100ml sunflower oil

1 tsp sesame oil

50ml rice vinegar

1 tbsp light soft brown sugar

½ red chilli, diced

1 tbsp black poppy seeds

1 bunch fresh coriander, finely chopped

Slice the cucumbers down the middle and scoop out the seeds with a teaspoon, then slice them again down the middle. Take a rolling pin and bash them flat, then cut on an angle into pieces about 1cm thick. Mix together the oils, vinegar, sugar and chilli and pour over the cucumbers, making sure they are evenly coated. Sprinkle over the black poppy seeds. Finish off with a handful of the chopped coriander.

Treats
and Snacks

The Deadline

Forty thousand words. Forty thousand words to write in less than a month. It made her feel ill when she thought about it. Nowadays, if she could manage five hundred words a day she considered it an achievement. And she didn't even write every day either. She needed her weekends off.

She was going to have to up her word count to two thousand a day at least. She had already moved her deadline three times. Her editor was being incredibly patient and understanding.

'It's not quite gelling,' Caroline told her, trying not to sound desperate. 'It will, because it always does. But I need a little more time.'

'Of course,' soothed Marisa. She was always calm, measured, professional. The best editor Caroline had worked with: even though Marisa only looked about twelve years old, she seemed to have a lifetime of knowledge about the human condition, as well as a deep

VERONICA HENRY

understanding of the creative process, which was not always the case with editors.

But even Marisa couldn't buy her any more time. The end of this month was the last possible date for Caroline to deliver if the book was going to be published this Christmas. There needed to be time to edit, polish, copyedit and proofread; fine-tune the cover and the copy; get it off to the printers – and then begin the process of reaching out to magazine and newspaper editors, book bloggers and influencers to make sure the book got into everyone's Secret Santa sack and Christmas stocking. Even with this schedule they were cutting it fine.

Luckily a novel by Caroline Talbot was usually a guaranteed success. She had hit that sweet spot. 'Wellwritten nonsense' was her trademark. She was a literary icon, even if she was never going to have literary acclaim. The Booker Prize had never been within her reach, but she didn't mind. She was no intellectual snob.

Besides, *The Misadventures of Tuesday DeVille* had done very nicely for her. This Christmas was going to be the thirtieth misadventure of the plucky, sparky, sexy private investigator who unravelled the murkier goings-on of pop stars, politicians and public figures in Swinging Sixties London. There was a big marketing budget waiting to be spent: posters at tube stations and on the sides of buses. But they needed a book first …

And there were plenty of other authors that money

could be spent on. Plenty of young talent waiting to wrest Caroline's crown from her. She was the reigning queen – the number one spot had belonged to her at Christmas for the past eight years – but she could easily be toppled.

Caroline had reached an impasse, though. Something deep inside her wanted something different for Tuesday; something more than stake-outs and honeytraps. Her heroine's age had stayed similar, a vague thirtysomething, in all the years she had been writing, and her readers seemed to accept that time stood still for the blonde in the white leather mac. In the last book, however, a grateful client had taken on greater importance than Caroline had anticipated. She knew she wanted Tuesday to fall in love with Angus Buchanan and his rambling mansion on the banks of a loch in the Scottish Highlands.

But that would mean the end of Tuesday's career. And perhaps, by association, Caroline's …

'I think,' said Calypso, her agent, over their last lunch at J. Sheekey, 'it's time for the Sin Bin.'

Caroline had looked down at her sea bass, her heart thumping. The Sin Bin was a beach hut on Everdene Sands, where Calypso sent clients who were struggling to write. Everyone knew the pressure was on for authors to deliver their very best, year after year, and sometimes it was hard. Sometimes the words didn't flow, the ideas didn't come. Calypso had bought the hut fifteen years ago, when there had been a flurry of sub-standard manuscripts from authors who were blocked and burnt-out. It had turned out to be a shrewd investment.

'I can't afford to lose a single manuscript,' Calypso told Caroline when she revealed her plan. 'This little hut will be the perfect retreat. There's nothing there but the sea, so there'll be no distractions. I'll arrange to have it stocked with each client's favourite food so they won't have to lift a finger while they're staying there. They can get away from it all, clear their heads, have a chance to stand back from their work. And then get some bloody words down so I can get my ten per cent.'

It had worked brilliantly. Dozens of her clients had taken advantage of the idyllic retreat, and the beach hut itself had doubled in value. Caroline had prided herself on never being banished there. Until now. This time she admitted defeat.

'I think you're right,' she sighed. 'But you're not to tell anyone.'

'It's always confidential. You know that,' said Calypso, signalling for the bill. 'You're not on any ridiculous diet, are you?'

Caroline raised an eyebrow and looked at her. 'No marzipan; no pickled eggs.'

Calypso laughed. 'I think we can manage that. I'll have everything ready for you.'

So here she was. And she had to admit that Calypso's retreat was the perfect place for a stressed-out writer. The hut was set slightly back from the others, protected by the undulating dunes. The sand was soft and golden; the sea crept in and out, switching from silver to turquoise to rose gold depending on the strength and position of the sun. The sunsets were breathtaking.

Inside, it was furnished with the last word in luxury. Everything was decorated in cream and pale turquoise – the agency colours. A desk stood at the window with the most comfortable ergonomic chair on the market. The bed on the mezzanine was a cloud of soft blankets and pillows, and above the bed was a shelf of classic beach reads, from *The Godfather* to *The Shell Seekers*. The fridge was packed with food that needed no preparation: bowls of homemade hummus and baba ghanoush; crab cakes to dip in chilli dipping sauce; fat golden pasties and jars of chutney. There were piles of fluffy beach towels and fleecy blankets. Noise-cancelling headphones. A sound system tuned to ambient music for maximum concentration. And, on the desk, a tin full of biscuits in the shape of beach huts, iced in blue and white.

But Calypso was no fool, either. There was no wi-fi, no television and no alcohol in the fridge. It was the most luxurious of prison cells.

Caroline set up her laptop at the table and laid out her precious notebook. She had a new one for each book – bright yellow leather, filled with featherlight paper and engraved with her initials – and in it she wrote all her ideas for characters and locations and plot twists, accompanied by pen-and-ink drawings. They were lined up on a bookshelf in her office at home, and she fancied that one day after her death they would be sold at auction for an eye-watering sum.

This notebook, however, was worryingly empty but for a drawing of a large Gothic mansion in front of a stretch of water. And pages of tartan. And a ring with an enormous sparkling blue sapphire. And a pair of deerhounds.

What on earth was the matter with her? The sketches were usually of E-type Jaguars, cocktail shakers, murky Soho coffee shops and strip clubs; record players and ashtrays; lipstick-stained cigarette ends and empty glasses. This was the world her readers loved: London in the 1960s. David Bailey, the Beatles, Twiggy, Profumo. High-energy, hard-edged, decadent. Brimming with criminal activity and sexy exploits. And, at the heart of it, the cool, calculating and classy Tuesday, pistol and lipstick at the ready in her handbag.

She felt a lurch of panic. If she didn't get her act together, there would be no book this Christmas and publication would be postponed. It would mean no money for another year. The more she thought about it, the more she panicked. It was a horrible feeling. Her brain felt muzzy and foggy. She would type two sentences and then come to a grinding halt. She was drowning in uncertainty. It was an unfamiliar feeling. Caroline Talbot never felt uncertain.

There had always been rumours that she was difficult. That she refused to let anyone interfere with her work. That she would demand the covers of her books be changed umpteen times. That her name had to be in letters twice the size of her title. That when she was on tour, she insisted on south-facing views and Ruinart champagne in her hotel room, and that any car picking her up had to have leather seats.

There was a grain of truth in the rumours. She would only let certain people have access to her work, and if a copy editor tried to change anything, they would get very short shrift.

And the demands weren't demands, they were preferences. If she was on tour, she liked things to be just so. If it was impossible, it didn't matter, as long as an effort had been made to please her. She was not unreasonable. She worked hard. And she always went the extra mile to be charming to her fans, who adored her. She remembered the names of the ones who turned up year after year. She was happy to chat endlessly to them. She was a consummate professional, so why shouldn't she have her favourite champagne at the end of a long evening? She only asked for a half-bottle, after all.

If she didn't get this book finished, she wouldn't be asking for champagne ever again. If she failed to deliver, her fans would find another source of reading pleasure and their memory of her would fade. She mustn't lose her nerve.

'Focus, Caroline,' she told herself sternly, staring at the screen and the flashing cursor.

Perhaps she would go for a swim? She couldn't remember the last time she had got in the sea in England. Perhaps as a small girl with her family? The water shimmered in front of her, a deep inviting blue, but it wouldn't have the warmth of the Caribbean where she was used to bathing on her annual holiday to St Lucia. Calypso had urged her to pack her swimming costume nevertheless.

'It's invigorating. You never come out feeling worse than when you went in. Of course, it's cold to start with, but you get used to it.'

She pulled out her polka-dot swimsuit. It had a skirt on it to hide her tummy and her thighs. Sitting at a desk for ten hours a day had done nothing for her figure. For a moment, she had a mental image of herself as a plump lady from a seaside postcard, spilling out of her costume. She'd go for a walk instead. Stretch her legs after the long drive.

She opened the door to find a young man standing on the step outside, about to knock, two bags at his feet.

'This is hut 72, right?' he said. He was slim, with messy shoulder-length blond hair and tortoiseshell sunglasses, wearing faded jeans, a striped long-sleeved t-shirt and baseball boots. And a gorgeous scent, redolent of moss and rain.

There was something familiar about him. Caroline frowned.

'Have you brought a delivery?' No doubt Calypso had thought of something to tempt out the muse.

'No. I'm supposed to be staying here. Are you the housekeeper?' He had a husky voice with a laconic northern accent. She couldn't quite identify which region but it wasn't unattractive.

Caroline drew herself up. 'I am not. I'm staying here. You must have the wrong hut.'

'I don't think so. Turquoise and white, I was told.'

'By whom?'

He blinked. 'Calypso Jones?'

'Oh dear.' Caroline sighed. 'Well, I'm afraid she must have double-booked. Calypso is marvellous but admin isn't her strong point. I'm so sorry you've had a wasted journey.'

He looked mutinous. 'I've got a deadline. She sent me to finish on pain of death. *You'll* have to go.' He looked more closely at Caroline. 'Wait a minute. You're Caroline Talbot.'

'Yes.' Caroline felt pleased that he had recognised her. She supposed she was quite distinctive, with her mane of blonde curls and blingy dress sense left over from the eighties. 'And you are?'

He looked surprised. 'Radar Mulligan?' he replied, in a tone that implied he never had to reveal his identity.

'Of course!' She recognised him now. He'd written the biggest hit of last year. The pretty boy whose gritty urban thriller had sold over half a million copies and was about to be made into a movie. She smoothed down her kaftan, turquoise, covered in hundreds of little mirrors. 'Oh dear. What are we going to do?'

'Well, I can't go home. I've come from Manchester, by train and taxi. I'll never get back tonight.'

Caroline checked her watch with a tut.

'I'll get Calypso to send a car for you. This is her fault for being so bloody disorganised. She'll have to sort it out. I've already unpacked.'

He took off his glasses and pushed back his hair. She saw his eyes: grey, with a dark ring around them.

'You don't understand. This is a crisis.' He indicated the laptop bag at his feet. 'My first draft's due in two weeks and it's a mess.'

He almost looked as if he might cry. Overnight success was, of course, a terrible strain. And following up a debut smash hit was an awful burden. There was nothing more inhibiting than a meteoric rise. He looked so crestfallen that Caroline relented.

'Come on in then. Let's have some tea and make a plan.'

Oh God. She sounded like his nanny. But he seemed to quite like being bossed about, and followed her in amiably.

'Wow. This place is pretty cool.' He looked around the hut and flopped down on the cream linen sofa, putting his feet up on the arm and his hands behind his head. She restrained herself from telling him to take off his shoes. She couldn't quite believe it. Here she was, rustling up tea for the *enfant terrible* of the literary scene. Unlike her, he'd had reviews in all the broadsheets, heralding him as the new Raymond Chandler with his whip-smart dialogue and intricate plotting. As well as being in the broadsheets he was in the tabloids too. He was the new best friend of actors and pop stars. There were queues of fangirls at his book signings. The Liam Gallagher of books, they called him, because he went out and partied hard with his groupies afterwards and had got into several fights on his tour. Though he looked angelic at the moment.

As she laid out scones, raspberry jam and rich, yellow clotted cream she was surprised by his appreciation.

'This looks amazing. Thank you so much. I'm starving,' he said.

'It's a proper Devon cream tea. Which means you have to put the cream on first.'

He looked at her. 'But of course,' he smiled, and she felt herself melt a little.

'Feet off the sofa,' she said, unable to stop herself swiping at his baseball boots and putting a plate down on the table in front of him. 'Shall I be mother?'

'Must you?' he asked, sitting up. 'I'd much rather you were just yourself.'

He was flirting with her. Cheeks pink, Caroline poured

the tea and reminded herself that she *was* actually old enough to be his mother. She cleared her throat.

'So. Why has Calypso sent you here?'

'Writer's block, I guess.' He laughed, spooning up a dollop of clotted cream. 'I'm stuck. Convinced I can't write for toffee. Terrified I'm going to have to give back my advance.'

'Good old imposter syndrome.' Caroline waved her scone in the air. 'It's all part of the process, darling. If you think you're a genius, that's the time to start worrying. You have to think you're rubbish in order to write better. There's no other way round it, I'm afraid.'

'Oh.' He frowned. 'So do you ever feel like you're rubbish?'

'Every time. Usually after about twenty thousand words, when I realise I've got another eighty to go and no plot.' She laughed. 'Why do you think writers are drunks, historically? Look at Hemingway. Look at Fitzgerald. Look at Chandler. And here's the thing.' She leaned forward. 'It's not supposed to be easy.'

'Oh.' He bit into his scone. 'Oh my God, this is so good. I've never had a cream tea before.'

'What?'

'They don't really serve them in the backstreets of Stockport.'

Caroline laughed. He was funny. Charming. Self-deprecating. Not the arrogant brat the press had made out.

'Well, fill your boots,' she said. 'I shouldn't have had one. A moment on the lips ...'

He flicked a glance over at her. 'You look all right to me.'

She blushed again.

'Anyway,' she said briskly, changing the subject. 'You've got to silence the voice in your head that tells you you're no good. You wrote the fastest-selling paperback of last year. That wasn't a fluke. You're a jolly good writer.'

'Oh.' Radar looked pleased. 'Did you read it, then?'

'In one day. It's terrific. You're a natural. You can always tell by the rhythm if people can really write. You pick the reader up and carry them along effortlessly.'

'Thank you.' He cleared his throat, awkward. 'Sorry, but I've never—'

Caroline laughed. 'Read one of mine? I wouldn't expect you to have. Don't worry at all.'

'Well,' he said. 'Thank you for the advice. But what are we going to do? I'm booked in here for a fortnight.'

There was silence for a moment. Caroline summed the situation up. She didn't want to send him packing. He'd made her laugh. Brought out something maternal in her. And something else a little sweeter.

'I suppose,' she said, 'you could sleep in the back room. It's more of a cupboard, really, but it's got a single bed in it.'

'That'd be wicked. I won't disturb you. You won't know I'm here.'

She pointed at him.

'You're to write two thousand words a day while you're here. No loud music and no mess. No smoking.'

'I'm as pure as the driven snow, me. Don't believe what you read in the press.' He widened his eyes.

He was making her flustered. Caroline Talbot was never flustered.

'Let's have a gin and tonic,' she said.

He tutted. 'Calypso said no drink.'

'Bollocks to that,' said Caroline, who'd brought her own bottle of Tanqueray, her preferred writing tipple, knowing full well her agent's draconian ways.

'Wow,' he said. 'Turns out you're the rebel, not me. I wouldn't have dared.'

Three drinks later and they were getting on famously. Caroline heated up the crab cakes chilling in the fridge before they forgot to eat and got too drunk.

'This is more than I've eaten in weeks,' said Radar. She could believe it. He was skinny as a rake.

When they'd finished, he offered to wash up, then made her a cup of tea.

'I make the best brew. And this will stop you having a hangover, guaranteed.'

They sat side by side with their mugs on the steps outside, and he asked her for more advice.

'Tell the story you want to tell,' Caroline urged him. 'Don't worry that it might not be as good as your first.

You've got a team that will make sure it's up to scratch. They won't let you go out there with your pants down.'

He laughed at that. 'Well, that's easy for you to say. How many have you written?'

'Thirty this year. If I get it done.' Caroline made a face.

'Is that why you're here?'

'I want to take my heroine in a new direction and I don't think my editor is going to be happy.'

'What about your readers, though? Will they be happy? Surely they're the ones who count?'

'I don't know …'

'You literally just told me to write the story I want to tell.' He turned and looked at her, raising his eyebrows. 'You should listen to your own advice.'

Caroline sighed. 'That's not always how it works. Not when you've got a franchise. Tuesday is a career girl. They won't want her married off.'

He drained the last of his tea, thoughtful, then set his mug down on the step.

'Why don't you do two endings, then?'

'What?'

He shrugged. 'The reader can choose whichever they prefer. Tuesday goes off into the sunset. Or Tuesday chooses her career. That way everyone's happy.'

'I can't do that.'

'Why not do something no one's expecting? Be disruptive. It won't affect the quality of your writing.'

'No …'

'Try it. Try it while we're here. What have you got to lose?' He leaned into her and she could smell him. Petrichor. That's what it was. The heady scent of rain on warm tarmac. 'Don't get stuck in your ways. Take a risk.'

She shut her eyes for a moment, breathing him in, knowing that whenever she smelled that smell in future she would picture him. 'Thank you, Radar,' she said, eventually. 'It's a brilliant idea. I'm going to try it.'

'Well, you've inspired me, so it's the least I can do.'

They smiled at each other. Caroline found herself blushing yet again as she met the deep grey of his eyes. And as their gazes locked, she suddenly realised something.

'The bloody manipulative old fox!' she said.

'Eh?'

'This was no accident,' she told him. 'We've been set up.'

Shrewd Calypso. She knew her clients so well. The old hand versus the new kid on the block, offering each other their wisdom.

Radar gave a mischievous chuckle, leaning back against the wall of the hut and crossing his arms. 'Right. Well. We're going to have to get our revenge, then, aren't we?'

'How are we going to do that?'

'The bloody paps have been on my back ever since the book came out. So let's give them something to write about. What do you reckon?'

'I don't follow.'

'We'll tip 'em off. Tell them that two chart-topping writers are shacked up on the beach together. They'll be here like a shot.'

'Do you think so?'

'Yeah. Especially if we can get J. K. Rowling to make it a threesome.' He grinned. 'I don't reckon it will do our sales any harm. And, let's face it, someone else will tip them off if we don't.'

'But would anyone believe it? You and me?'

He looked at her, that grey gaze sweeping her up and down. 'Why wouldn't they?' he said softly.

The next morning, Caroline piled her blonde curls on top of her head, put on her glitziest leopard-print kaftan and a swipe of red lipstick. Not bad, she thought, checking herself out in the mirror. She might be carrying a few extra pounds but she could still pull it out of the bag. Radar grinned at her. He was in cut-off shorts and a *Trainspotting* t-shirt.

'Come on, then, darling.' He took her hand, and they opened the door to the hut and stepped outside into the sunshine. They feigned surprise at the cluster of photographers who had set themselves up on the beach outside.

'Got anything to say about this?' shouted one of them.

'It's an interesting new chapter,' drawled Caroline, snaking her arm around Radar's neck and resting her head on his shoulder.

'It's a twist I didn't see coming,' said Radar, planting an affectionate kiss on her cheek.

'But is it happy ever after?' shouted another.

They weren't going to be drawn any longer.

'We'd be grateful if you'd leave us alone now,' said Radar. 'We've both got work to do.'

They posed for a few more photographs then stepped back inside the hut and closed the door. For a moment they collapsed onto each other, laughing.

'They totally fell for it,' wheezed Radar.

'I know. Imagine!'

He stopped laughing and looked at her for a moment. 'Yeah,' he said. 'I am.'

His hand was still on her arm. She didn't know what to say. It wasn't fair of him to tease her. She stepped away from the heat of his fingers.

'Right,' she said. 'I'll do coffee and scrambled eggs. Then it's straight down to it. You don't get lunch until you've written a thousand words.'

'Bloody hell,' grumbled Radar. 'It's like boot camp.'

'It certainly is.'

'I bet you won't let me have a beer either, will you?'

She raised an eyebrow. 'Not until six.'

The day passed in a blur. The two of them sat opposite each other, fingers racing over their keyboards, sustained by jugs of *agua fresca* and chocolate chip cookies. By evening, they had each written over three thousand words and could see the road ahead.

'I'd never have done this without you,' said Radar. 'I'd've sat here with my head in my hands, bellyaching.'

'Well, you've helped me too. Tuesday's mistress of the big house by the loch and it feels like the right place for her. I'm going to leave her there, then create a new character, for a new series. Someone a little older and wiser.'

'There's definitely magic in this air,' he said, looking outside to the late afternoon sun dancing on the waves, strewing golden beads of light across the water.

Caroline shut her laptop lid. 'Calypso's a clever old bird.'

They sat there in companionable silence, both relishing the satisfaction of a hard day's work combined with the prospect of a pleasant evening ahead. The hut was filled with a soft light, and the sea air danced in through the door.

'I don't know about you, but I'm starving,' said Caroline.

Radar walked over to the kitchen and peered into the fridge. 'Pasties and baked beans do you? I can just about manage that without burning it.'

'Perfect,' said Caroline, thinking that truth really was stranger than fiction. In her wildest dreams she would never have imagined wild boy Radar Mulligan cooking dinner for her.

You couldn't make it up.

TREATS AND SNACKS

❋

*T*here isn't a writer I know who doesn't take themselves off for a few days from time to time for some uninterrupted writing. To wake in the morning and be able to dive straight into work is a real luxury, but it can also be a necessity. Sometimes you need the space to get your head around the plot, work out all the backstories, untangle all the complications and find a path through to the end. Getting away from it all is the only answer, although it's not always that easy.

But even more than a writing retreat, I often long for a reading retreat. Even though it's part of my job to keep up with all the latest bestsellers, there never seems to be time to do them justice. The thought of having nothing else to worry about for a whole week, and then to lie in the sun with a book – with perhaps the occasional dip in the sea when it gets too warm – seems like paradise.

I'm sure it's not just writers who long for that indulgence. We all have books tucked away we haven't read yet, or old favourites we long to return to. And juggling work and family and everyday life means we usually only get time for a paragraph or two before our eyes find themselves closing.

And to really lose yourself between the pages, it's vital not to be troubled by the day-to-day minutiae, or to have to worry about what to cook, so the fridge must be well stocked. Clever Calypso, to provide such toothsome indulgence for Caroline and Radar!

Agua fresca

This is perfect to make in the morning and keep in a jug to sip at all day long.

MAKES 6 GLASSES

¼ small watermelon (about 450g of flesh)

200g fresh raspberries

Juice of 2 limes

1 litre chilled water

2 tsp honey, or to taste (optional)

6 fresh mint sprigs

Roughly chop the watermelon flesh and add to a food processor along with the raspberries and lime juice. Pour in the water and whizz until pulverised. This makes a refreshingly tart drink, but if you prefer it sweeter add a little honey when whizzing. Strain through a fine sieve into a jug, discarding the pulp. Add a sprig of mint to your glass before pouring.

Crostini

Crostini are ideal to serve with dips and pâtés. This recipe is super-quick and easy and makes the perfect base for the toppings that follow. All of these are perfect for that time of day when everyone is a little peckish but it's not quite time for lunch. Ideal with a little bottle of beer or a splash of white wine – day time drinking is allowed at the seaside, after all.

MAKES 30–40 CROSTINI

1 baguette

Olive oil

Preheat the oven to 190°C/fan 170°C/gas mark 5. Cut the baguette into very thin slices. Place them in a baking tray and drizzle liberally with olive oil then bake for 10 minutes, turning once, until they are lightly toasted. Keep a sharp eye on them as they can go from golden brown to burnt very quickly!

The crostini will keep in a tin for a couple of days, but if you make any of the following they will disappear pretty quickly.

Smoked mackerel pâté

This is the archetypal minimum effort, maximum impact creation. I always forget about it, and then when I remember and make it I'm amazed all over again at how delicious it is. It is very rich, though, so don't spoil your lunch!

SERVES 4 TO GO WITH DRINKS

4 mackerel fillets (about 300g), skins removed

1 × 180g tub cream cheese

Zest and juice of 1 lemon

1 tsp horseradish or dash of Tabasco sauce

Cayenne pepper

Baby cornichons

Use a fork to break up the mackerel flesh. Put in a food processor with the cream cheese, the lemon zest and juice and the horseradish. Whizz until smooth. You might need to scrape down the sides halfway through. Put into a bowl, smooth over the top, add a sprinkling of cayenne pepper and an extra squeeze of lemon juice. Serve on brown toast, topped with the halved baby cornichons.

Spicy garlicky olive oil

My great friend Alice taught me this trick: a spicy garlicky oil for making hummus or baba ghanoush (see below). By heating the oil first then turning it off and letting the garlic and spices infuse there is less danger of them burning, and the flavours really develop.

2 tbsp olive oil
2 garlic cloves, roughly chopped
1 tsp cumin seeds
1 tsp fennel seeds
Strips of lemon peel
1 tsp sea salt

Heat the oil in a heavy-bottomed pan then turn off the heat. Add the garlic, spices, lemon peel and salt, and leave in the oil for a couple of hours to infuse.

Hummus

What is it about hummus that inspires such passion? Its ingredients are very unprepossessing, nor does it look particularly appetising, but it's always received with rapturous delight and devoured within seconds. And it's the easiest thing to make if people turn up unexpectedly – always keep a tin of chickpeas on the shelf.

SERVES 4 TO GO WITH DRINKS

1 × 400g tin chickpeas, drained
1 quantity Spicy Garlicky Olive Oil (see p.108)
Zest and juice of 1 lemon
1 tbsp olive oil
2 tbsp tahini
1 tbsp pine kernels, lightly toasted
1 tbsp chopped coriander
Sea salt and freshly ground black pepper

Put the chickpeas in a food processor with the infused oil, lemon zest and juice, olive oil and tahini. Whizz to a smooth paste. Taste and season with salt and pepper, and add a little extra olive oil if the mixture is too dry. Serve in a bowl, garnished with a few lightly toasted pine kernels and some fresh coriander.

Baba ghanoush

Baba ghanoush means 'spoiled dad', and its creamy smoky softness is out of this world. In fact, the French call it *caviar d'aubergines*, which is quite a name to live up to. I think it does! It's weirdly addictive.

SERVES 4 TO GO WITH DRINKS

2 large aubergines, pricked all over
1 quantity Spicy Garlicky Olive Oil (see p.108)
Zest and juice of 1 lemon
1 tbsp tahini
Sea salt, to taste

Preheat the oven to 220°C/fan 200°C/gas mark 7 and roast the aubergines until they are really soft when poked with a knife – up to 1½ hours, but keep checking on them.

Remove the skins and put the flesh in a food processor with the infused oil, the lemon zest and juice and the tahini. Whizz to a smooth paste, adding salt if needed.

OTHER CROSTINI TOPPINGS:

- Boursin cheese and a couple of slices of roasted red peppers.

- Cream cheese and smoked salmon.

- Tapenade and a slice of goat's cheese.

- Rare roast beef on mayonnaise with rocket.

- Thinly sliced radishes on unsalted butter.

Crab cakes with sweetcorn salsa

The perfect light lunch that won't make you want to fall asleep – though you are very welcome to, of course. If you don't want to bother with making the salsa then the crab cakes are great dunked into sweet chilli dipping sauce.

SERVES 2

1 garlic clove

1 small piece fresh ginger (about 2cm)

½ tsp sea salt

300g fresh white crab meat or 200g minced fresh prawns

Zest and juice of 1 lime

100g breadcrumbs

1 large egg, whisked

Sunflower oil, for frying

Sweet chilli dipping sauce (optional)

For the sweetcorn salsa

1 × 326g tin sweetcorn, drained

2 large beef tomatoes, deseeded and chopped

1 avocado, finely diced

1 red chilli, thinly sliced

Zest and juice of I lime
Sea salt and freshly ground black pepper
2 tbsp chopped coriander

First, make the salsa. Tip the sweetcorn into a bowl and add the tomatoes, avocado and chilli. Mix together and add the lime zest and juice. Season with salt and pepper, and stir through half the chopped coriander, sprinkling the rest on top. Set aside while you make the crab cakes.

Chop the garlic and ginger together very finely and mix with the salt. Stir into the crab or prawns with the lime zest and juice. Stir in the breadcrumbs and just enough egg to bring the mixture together. Divide into small patties about 5 cm across. Heat about 5mm oil in a frying pan and cook for 2 minutes on each side.

Serve the crab cakes with the sweetcorn salsa, or with chilli dipping sauce if you prefer.

Traditional pasty

This is the ultimate traditional beach lunch in the South West.
We buy them from the pasty shop, piping hot in a paper bag,
and we each have our own favourite flavour – but they are
super-easy to make yourself. It's important to dice everything
into small, even pieces to enable it all to cook through
properly.

MAKES 4 PASTIES

500g ready-made shortcrust pastry
1 onion, finely diced
250g carrot, finely diced
400g potato, finely diced
400g sirloin steak, cut into very small pieces
Dash of Worcester sauce
Sea salt and freshly ground black pepper
1 egg, beaten

Preheat the oven to 220°C/fan 200°C/gas mark 7 and grease
a baking sheet.

Roll out the pastry and cut into four equal 22cm circles,
about the size of a side plate. Mix together the vegetables,

meat and Worcester sauce and season well with salt and pepper. Spoon a quarter of the meat and veg mix down the centre of each circle. Dampen the edges of each circle with a little water and draw the sides together, crimping the edges with your fingers to make a firm seal so the pasty has a little spine (this was what the tin miners used to grab hold of so they didn't get their pasty grubby). Brush with the beaten egg and put a small hole in each pasty with the tip of a knife to let out the steam. You can, if you're feeling whimsical, make a pastry initial with the leftover pastry for each person.

Transfer to the baking sheet and cook for 10 minutes then reduce the oven to 150°C/fan 130°C/gas mark 2 and bake for another 30 minutes.

OTHER FLAVOUR SUGGESTIONS

- Potato and onion

- Broccoli and Stilton

- Chicken and mushroom

- Ham and leek

- Sausage and apple

A twist on a traditional cream tea

You can't go to the seaside without indulging in a cream tea. You just can't. And it's best to bake your own scones, because then you can make them the exact size you like, add whatever fruit you fancy and know that they are fresh out of the oven that day. Source and buy the richest, yellowest local clotted cream you can find and bring along your favourite jam. For me, it's raspberry every time, as raspberries taste of summer and my Irish grandmother's garden. And I don't really care whether you are cream first or jam first – it's delicious whichever way you slosh it on! But, for the record, I'm cream first. That's because I live in Devon. Devon: cream first. Cornwall: jam first. Try both!!

It's easy enough to find a scone recipe – you can count on Mary Berry or Delia Smith, for example – so I'm sharing with you an experiment. While writing this book I had the most delicious experience in the tea room of a garden near to me: ginger scones with cream and honey. It was one of those gastronomic epiphanies that don't happen very often: something so simple and obvious yet I'd never come across the combination before. I dreamed of it for days afterwards and then decided to make my own.

MAKES 8 SCONES

225g self-raising flour, plus extra for dusting

1 tsp sea salt

60g butter, cut into small dice

30g sugar

1 tsp ground ginger

2 balls of stem ginger, very finely chopped

100ml milk

Clotted cream

Honey

Preheat the oven to 220°C/fan 200°C/gas mark 7 and flour or line a baking sheet with parchment paper.

Sift the flour and salt into a large bowl. Add the butter and stir in with a knife until the lumps are coated, then rub gently into the flour with your fingers until it resembles fine

breadcrumbs and there are no lumps left. Stir in the sugar and gingers. Add the milk and stir with a knife or a wooden spoon until everything begins to draw together and you have a ball of dough.

Lift onto a floured surface. Pat or roll the dough out to a thickness of about 2.5cm. Cut out rounds using a cutter – you must keep the edges sharp and not twist, to get the best rise. Re-roll the excess dough until you have used it all up. You can dust the tops with flour, or brush a little milk or beaten egg on the surface if you want shiny scones.

Place the scones on the baking sheet and cook for 8–10 minutes – they should feel nice and light when you lift them up. As they have ginger in them they will look a little more golden than usual scones. Cool and eat as soon after baking as you can. Split them open and top with the clotted cream and a spoonful of honey

Sea salt chocolate chip cookies

These cookies are the perfect treat to nibble on while you are reading. It could be possible to eat them all yourself …

If you can't find sea salt chocolate, simply buy plain chocolate and then scatter the cookies with sea salt just before baking.

MAKES ABOUT 16 COOKIES

150g sea salt chocolate

125g softened butter

125g light soft brown sugar

1 large egg, beaten

1 tsp vanilla extract

150g plain flour, sifted

½ tsp baking powder

Preheat the oven to 190°C/fan 170°C/gas mark 5 and grease two baking sheets.

Chop up the chocolate into little chips with a sharp knife. Cream together the butter and sugar until light and fluffy, then add the egg and vanilla extract. Gradually stir in the flour and baking powder then add the chocolate chips but do NOT overmix.

Dollop small walnut-sized spoonfuls of the mix onto the baking sheets, leaving plenty of room as they will spread. Bake for around 12–15 minutes until they are just turning golden, keeping a sharp eye so they don't burn.

Let them cool slightly and then remove to a wire cooling rack.

TEN CLASSIC
BEACH READS

Every good beach hut should have a shelf full of well-thumbed beach reads for the visitor to plunder. 'Beach read' doesn't necessarily mean trashy but the idea is to relax and enjoy what you are reading and to give your brain a holiday. I call this kind of book 'brain candy' – the literary equivalent of a Magnum: quality ingredients, indulgent, delicious.

For me, the best beach read has to be a decent size, page-turning and completely immersive so I can lose myself and become oblivious to what's going on around me (often to the annoyance of anyone trying to grab my attention). It should take me to another place yet it shouldn't be too demanding – I should be able to race through the pages effortlessly. This means a combination of vivid description, engaging characters and gripping plots.

This is a list of my favourite beach reads – a mixture

of romantic, blockbusting, thrilling and historic. My copies of these are battered, torn and yellowed. Some are classics in the old-fashioned sense of the word. Others are timeless blockbusters – or bonkbusters, as the more racy are known! All are unputdownable, except to pour a cup of tea or fetch an ice cream.

The Godfather – MARIO PUZO

I found this on my parents' bookshelf when I was about twelve and read it with wide eyes and an open mouth. Sicilian mafia shenanigans with the Corleone family – sexy, ruthless, fast-paced drama with some unforgettable scenes and lines: poor old Luca Brasi, sleeping with the fishes!

Jaws – PETER BENCHLEY

I bought this at the airport when I was heading back to boarding school from America where we'd been posted. It certainly kept me engrossed on the flight. Small-town politics and sexual liaisons underpin the arrival of a great white shark to an idyllic coastal resort. It's pretty raunchy – I kept my room-mates enthralled reading out the rude bits!!

Valley of the Dolls – JACQUELINE SUSANN

This was the original bonkbuster and paved the way for commercial women's fiction, sex and shopping, chicklit – call it what you will. Shocking at the time, it is the tautly plotted and eye-opening tale of three successful women in showbusiness and their slide into dependence on uppers and downers – the 'dolls' of the title.

Riders – JILLY COOPER

Jilly Cooper is the ultimate in escapism with her outrageous, larger-than-life but lovable characters and their gorgeous rambling houses. The Olympic show-jumping team are rivals for more than just medals – love, lust and legs in tight jodhpurs. Naughty but incredibly nice!

Scruples – JUDITH KRANTZ

Sharp, witty and sexy, Judith Krantz's stylish blockbusters were the archetypal sex and shopping novels in the 1980s. *Scruples* is a classic as Billy Winthrop evolves from overweight nobody to the glamorous owner of a top Hollywood boutique.

Destiny – SALLY BEAUMAN

Sally hit the literary headlines when she got the first million-pound book deal for this sweeping story of star-crossed love spanning several decades and continents. It's rich, deep and multi-layered, and extremely classy writing.

Lace – SHIRLEY CONRAN

Superwoman Shirley Conran is the queen of one-liners – not least 'life's too short to stuff a mushroom'. Labyrinthine plotting explores the friendship of four strong women – sex, sin, scandal and revenge.

Cashelmara – SUSAN HOWATCH

I love anything in a windswept Irish setting, and this is the cream of the crop. Starting in 1869, three generations of the de Salis family play out their dramas in a breathtaking Irish house, Cashelmara. It's a fascinating insight into the Irish famine told from six different points of view.

The Shell Seekers – ROSAMUNDE PILCHER

Rosamunde Pilcher indisputably rules contemporary Cornish fiction, bringing the seaside to life through her romantic bestsellers, and this is the most famous. When a mother is put under pressure by her children to sell a beloved family painting, *The Shell Seekers*, everything starts to go wrong.

Quentins – MAEVE BINCHY

Whenever I go on holiday, there is always a Maeve Binchy in the cottage, the B&B or the hotel library where I'm staying, which is a testament to her enduring storytelling and universal popularity. This is the most wonderfully satisfying of her books, featuring the stories behind the staff and customers of a legendary Dublin restaurant.

A birthday banquet

A Fair Exchange

JUNE 1968

'Come on, girly. Chop chop.' Dickon Travers gestured towards the Triumph Herald waiting on the pavement, but showed no sign of helping Elspeth with the picnic basket she was carrying. He was only chivalrous when it suited him, she'd noticed; only chivalrous when other people were looking.

She opened her mouth to remind him of her name for the umpteenth time when his arms shot up in the air and he started waving to another motor car trundling along the road, a rather less glamorous Morris Minor Traveller. It mounted the pavement outside the college and came to a halt behind his. The streets of Oxford were still quiet. It was far too early on a summer Sunday for activity, even if the sun was already up and about.

'Hey! Here you are! Terrific.' Dickon greeted the inmates of the car then turned back to Elspeth and hurried over, scooping up the basket in his arms and lugging it round to the boot. 'You didn't forget the cake?' he hissed as he went to slam down the lid.

'Of course not.' For a moment, she debated not coming. He'd been showing his true colours in the past few weeks, and she didn't much care for them. He was all bluster, and his affable charm didn't go very deep. But if she backed out now there would be a scene. It was going to be a gloriously warm day, and a trip to the seaside was tempting. It was Dickon and his twin sister Octavia's birthday, and they were all heading down to Devon, to the Travers family beach hut. Six of them. A day of games, a birthday banquet, lashings of booze.

It should be fun. Elspeth felt nervous, nevertheless. These were not her people, not really. She'd been dazzled by Dickon at first. Flattered that he found her so intriguing when it was very obvious she wasn't one of his kind. She was ordinary. A grammar-school girl who had worked her socks off to get to Oxford, not like the Travers twins for whom it was a given.

She was just a novelty to Dickon, she knew that. Of course, she was very clever, although that didn't make you stand out at Oxford. But she was beautiful too, unusually so, with thick dark wavy hair and navy-blue eyes, very tall and slim. Her height made her self-conscious. She felt gangly next to most girls, and longed to be petite and dainty. Her arms seemed too long for any of her blouses, and she thought her knees knobbly. But people – men –

seemed taken with her. Her looks seemed to be a ticket, even if she didn't always have the confidence to go where that ticket took her.

Maybe the confidence would come. Her mother told her never to be afraid of anyone, her tiny little spitfire of a mum who was so proud yet so scared for her. She had been very quiet the day they went to Oxford to look around, awed by the grandeur of the buildings, the hallowed atmosphere. And disconcerted by the aura of all the people who swept through the streets. People who would never notice a little grey-haired woman from Stoke-on-Trent scurrying along the pavement beside her leggy daughter.

It had rained, and when her mum had pulled her see-through rain hood out of her bag and snapped the popper tight under her chin, Elspeth had been overwhelmed with love for the widow who had done everything she could for her daughter. She couldn't bear the thought of leaving her, but leave her she must, for Elspeth was no fool. She didn't want to stay in Stoke for the rest of her life, and Oxford was the fastest route out. The applause of prize-giving still rang in her ears. She could still feel the warm handshake of the headmistress. Her name was written in gold on the wall of the dining hall. All those hours in the library had paid off. She was daunted but she loved her subject and had been happy to immerse herself. She might, one day, be an historian in her own right.

And now, her first year had come to an end and she still felt something of a fish out of water. Even though she loved her studies and had kept on top of them, taking them far more seriously than most of her contemporaries. Around her, there was a lot of drinking, a lot of acting, a lot of poetry. And a lot of sex.

She had met Dickon at the college tennis club. Tennis was the other thing she had excelled at, and it had proven a very useful way to meet people in a setting where she felt comfortable. She was happy in front of the net, racquet in hand. She understood the geography of a tennis court and was much happier there than in the pub or the JCR. The Travers twins were the stars of the club, ruthlessly competitive while pretending not to be, their blond heads flashing and their pale-blue eyes not missing a shot.

Elspeth always had the feeling that if she had beaten Octavia in a match, something bad would happen to her. Luckily, she didn't care enough to put it to the test. She played for pleasure. She'd been put with Dickon in a mixed doubles tournament, and he'd been impressed enough with her game to ask her for a drink afterwards. And somehow, she was now his girlfriend. She felt certain it was only so he could make some other girl jealous. He couldn't possibly have any real interest in her. Could he? She'd never been hunting, or skiing. She didn't have any family silver, or portraits, or a house in the country.

She thought she understood how Charles Ryder had

once felt, thrust among those gilded Flytes, though the Travers family were neither Catholic nor had a home as stately as Brideshead. Elspeth had read as many books about Oxford as she could before she went up, to familiarise herself with the way of life and prepare herself. *Zuleika Dobson*, *Jude the Obscure* – none of them really made her feel comfortable with what she was about to experience, except *Gaudy Night* by Dorothy L. Sayers, which she'd loved, and had made her feel she was doing the right thing, that it was okay for an ordinary girl to aim high.

The fact that Dickon called her 'girly', or 'bird', or 'totty', proved to her he wasn't really that keen. She was getting tired of him. He turned the charm on and off like a tap. He was best when he'd just won a match and had only a couple of drinks. Then he was funny and warm – affectionate, even – and she found herself drawn to him. But any more drinks and he became belligerent. His face got red, his voice got louder and she found herself recoiling. As they clambered into his car, she wondered again if this was a good idea. Was it too late to tell him she felt ill?

And then she saw Harry Moore getting out of the Morris to check a tyre. She had played against him once or twice in mixed doubles. You could tell a lot about a person by how they played tennis. He was relaxed, easy, confident. Pulled it out of the bag if he had to, but didn't get het up if he lost a point. He'd complimented her on her serve. 'You should join the university team,' he told her, but she wasn't cut-throat enough. She knew that.

Knowing he was coming to the hut too reassured her. He didn't have the frenzied hedonism of the usual Travers set. He wasn't dull, by any means, but there was a solidity about him that was definitely lacking in Dickon. And he was extremely handsome. He had the sort of face it was a pleasure to rest your eyes on. Russet hair and eyes that crinkled when he laughed and skin that turned pale gold in the sun.

Octavia was needling Harry to get back in the car. 'We'll never get there in time!' It was a miracle they were on the road by seven in the morning, given how much they'd all drunk the night before. Elspeth hadn't had nearly as much as most of them, but she was still a bit queasy, though she felt more settled knowing Harry was coming to the beach.

Her and Dickon. Octavia and Harry. And Rory Gill and his girlfriend Juliet, the girl Elspeth felt sure Dickon had his eye on and was trying to impress. Juliet was aloof, with very short black hair and a Roman nose, and she chain-smoked.

'She's a lady,' Octavia told her, and it took Elspeth a while to realise she meant a Lady, that it was a title, and she thought that probably explained a lot.

She wasn't going to tell any of them she had never been to the seaside. She could only imagine their cries of disbelief. She and her mother lived in landlocked Stoke. They had no car. No money for luxuries like a holiday. She wished for a moment that her mum was with her. Not with this crowd, though. Just the two of them. One day, when she'd left university and got a proper job, she would take her mother to a beautiful hotel, with a private bathroom and a dining room overlooking the sea.

She slept for most of the journey. She found Dickon's driving quite alarming, so she preferred to have her eyes closed. But towards lunchtime he nudged her awake.

'Look!' he cried.

They were driving down a steep hill, and at the bottom she could see a vast stretch of sparkling blue water, the sun high in a cloudless sky above. She didn't know what to say. Her first view of the sea. She knew she would never forget it.

'Oh,' was all she could manage. Everything was different here. The light. The air. As if they were one step closer to paradise.

'My favourite place in the world,' said Dickon, softly. 'Nothing seems to matter here.'

She looked at him and thought she saw the glitter of tears in his eyes. Perhaps he wasn't such a bad person. He obviously felt deeply about this place and she could quite see why. She felt a little overwhelmed herself. Light-headed, light-hearted. The two of them laughed as the car sped down the hill, the wind in their hair.

If the sea was a revelation, the beach hut was a delight. There were just a few of them at the foot of the dunes on Everdene Sands, glorified sheds where families shacked up and stored their things. The one belonging to the Travers family had a rickety veranda at the front and was painted pale green. Inside were a couple of bunk beds, some old chairs, a gas ring and a cupboard with plates and mugs and bowls. It smelled of damp salt.

'We camp out here every summer,' Octavia told Elspeth. The others had arrived not long after them. 'It's heaven. All we do is swim and read and sleep.'

'Last one in the sea's a rotten egg,' said Dickon, who was peeling off his clothes. Elspeth looked alarmed. He obviously had every intention of going in naked. There was no one else on this part of the beach. She had taken the precaution of buying herself a swimming costume the day before, when she knew they were heading to the coast, but she didn't want to get changed in front of all the others.

'There's no point in being shy,' Juliet drawled, noticing her discomfort and blowing out a plume of cigarette smoke. 'This lot strip off at any opportunity.'

Elspeth managed to shimmy into her costume underneath her dress, then raced along the sand to the water's edge. She stretched out her arms as if to embrace the view, overwhelmed by all the sensations: the sea breeze kissing her skin, the brackish smell of salt in the air, the icy water lapping at her feet. It was glorious, and she yelped with excitement as she waded into the waves, gasping as they leapt up at her. Dickon was already on his back gazing at the sky. Harry bounded in beside her and dived straight under, coming up with his hair slicked back, and Elspeth felt a bit funny when she looked at his lean physique next to Dickon's pale roundness. Dickon wasn't fat as such, just … soft. She found herself wondering what firmer flesh might feel like, and had to dive under the water to wash her thoughts away.

Lunch was lavish and too rich. Elspeth looked in doubt at the platter of lobster, not sure it had benefited from being shut up in the car boot for hours on a hot day, but the twins ripped them apart eagerly and served them up with several bottles of white wine. The cake she had brought, a Victoria sponge filled with cream and jam, seemed very plain in comparison, but it disappeared rapidly enough.

By mid-afternoon they were all collapsed on rugs in front of the hut. Octavia rested her head on Harry's chest, and Elspeth felt a dart of jealousy as sharp as a jellyfish sting. The two of them had exchanged bemused glances once or twice throughout lunch at the air of debauchery and overindulgence and she felt allied with him. When Dickon opened a bottle of champagne to toast their birthday, Harry winked at her almost imperceptibly and she felt her pulse quicken. They were conspirators; the arbiters of good sense and restraint amid the decadent profligacy.

Dickon was running his hand up and down her bare calf, and she felt tense at his touch, especially as she could see he was staring at Juliet behind his sunglasses. Wine emboldened her, and she jumped up.

'Come on, everyone,' she cried. 'Let's do a human pyramid.'

They all seemed to think this was a brilliant idea.

'Who goes on the top, though?' asked Dickon.

'Not me,' said Juliet. 'No fear.'

'Whoever is lightest, surely?' said Octavia.

Everyone looked at Elspeth, who despite being the tallest was also the slimmest. 'I don't mind,' she said, wanting to impress Harry with her gameness. She had always been pretty good at gymnastics and had a sense of balance, and the pyramid would only be three people high.

It seemed to take forever to assemble the pyramid, with the three men on all fours at the bottom, then Octavia and Juliet kneeling on top of them. They made a terrible fuss as Elspeth scrambled up, though she tried not to dig her toes in. Eventually she stood on their shoulders, spreading out her arms. Dickon had persuaded someone from the neighbouring hut to take a photograph, and she struggled to maintain her balance while they all said 'cheese'.

Then Dickon, far drunker than the rest, thought it

would be funny to rear up like a circus horse, lifting his hands off the ground and pawing the air with a neigh. Octavia and Juliet shrieked and everyone came tumbling down in a big heap. Elspeth tried desperately to keep her balance, but it was impossible. She felt herself toppling, and tried to roll herself up like she'd been taught in gymnastics, but she landed with her leg underneath her and cried out.

'You idiot,' Harry said to Dickon, furious. 'What the hell was that for, you buffoon?'

'Trust Dickon to ruin it,' said Octavia. 'Are you all right, Elspeth?'

'I'm not sure.' Elspeth had gone slightly green from too much wine, sun and the pain. 'It hurts.'

'Try to move it.'

'I can't. Oh. Ow.' And to her embarrassment, she was sick in the sand. Lobster and cake and champagne.

'Oh, God,' said Dickon. 'I can't stand puke.'

'It was your fault,' said Harry, glaring at him.

'It was her bloody idea.' Dickon kicked at the sand to cover the evidence.

Elspeth felt miserable. This wasn't how she'd intended the caper to turn out. She'd wanted to show off and now she thought she might have broken her ankle. These people were awful, she decided. She longed for home. For her mother. For her own bed. She started to shiver, even though it was still hot in the late afternoon sun.

'Let me feel,' said Harry, bending down and taking her ankle in his warm, brown hands. 'How does it feel? Can you walk on it?'

She tried to put her foot down but she couldn't bear her own weight. Maybe she should pretend it was all right. The sooner they got back to Oxford, the better.

'I think I should take you to hospital,' said Harry, pulling on his shirt. Dickon was in no fit state to play ambulance driver. He was slurring and swaying.

'I think you'd better.' Elspeth was near to tears. 'I'm so sorry to be a nuisance.'

'It's not your fault Dickon's such a clot.'

'But what if they keep her in? How are we all going to get back, if you take your car?' protested Octavia.

'We'll swap,' said Harry. 'You can all go back in the Morris, and I'll take the Triumph. I can bring Elspeth back to Oxford when she's been seen to.'

Dickon wasn't very happy about the car swap, but as the accident had been down to him he had little choice but to hand over his keys. Harry gave his to Juliet, who hadn't drunk as much as the rest of them. 'You drive,' he told her. 'Whatever you do, don't let Dickon behind the wheel.'

'We'll be here for a while yet. I'll be fine,' Juliet promised.

Then Harry bent down and lifted Elspeth into his arms. She protested, but she was never going to get to the car otherwise. He strode across the sand as if she weighed no more than a bag of sugar. She rested her head on his shoulder, feeling giddy, not sure if it was due to the strange turn of events or the heat from his chest.

It took half an hour to get to the hospital, where she was seen quickly. The ankle was just a sprain, and it was bandaged up tightly, and Elspeth was given a pair of crutches to help her walk for the next few days.

Back in the car, she looked at Harry. 'You've been so kind,' she said. 'Thank you. Thank you for looking after me.' She felt tearful, and homesick.

Harry was staring at the road ahead. 'Well, I don't think Dickon looks after you.'

'No,' said Elspeth. 'Not really.'

'You deserve much better.'

'Maybe.' Elspeth was dreading getting back to the hut and seeing them. Dickon mooning after Juliet. Juliet fully aware but feigning oblivion.

Harry said nothing, but after a while he held out his left hand, the palm outstretched, and she took it, wordlessly, and held onto it until he needed to change gear. And they carried on holding hands until they got back to the beach to see the Morris had gone.

'They've left already,' said Elspeth, not in the least bit sorry.

'What a shame,' said Harry, and smiled.

The two of them looked out to sea, where the sun was about to kiss the water, shimmering in a blaze of gilded coral.

'Do you know,' said Elspeth, 'I'd never been to the seaside before today.'

Harry put an arm around her shoulder. He didn't mock her.

'Well,' he said, 'in that case, it seems a pity to leave. Let's stay for the night. You haven't lived unless you've seen the sun rise over the sea.'

The implications of what he was saying sank in. Elspeth swallowed.

'What about Octavia?' she asked in a small voice.

Harry gave a dismissive gesture. 'There's nothing much between us. I'm not nearly landed enough for her. Far too ordinary.'

'You're not ordinary,' said Elspeth, fierce, for he wasn't. 'Won't they mind us sleeping in the hut?'

There was a small silence. The sun slipped further over the horizon. The sea was on fire.

'As a matter of fact,' said Harry, 'it's not their hut. Not any more.'

'What?' Elspeth turned to him, surprised.

Harry looked rueful. 'There's a lot you don't know about Dickon. Some of the people he's in with at Oxford are pretty wild. There's a lot of gambling. The stakes are high. He's lost a lot of money.'

'Oh.' Elspeth had heard there were clubs who indulged in reckless behaviour. Mostly rich males who behaved exactly as they pleased.

'I've tried time and again to help him stop, but he doesn't listen,' said Harry. 'And he can't afford to lose money. The twins like to pretend they're terribly wealthy, but there's not all that much family money.' He looked awkward. 'Anyway, Dickon came to me last week. He asked if I'd buy the hut off him. It's his, apparently. His granny left it to him.'

'I can't believe it,' said Elspeth. 'Actually, no – I *can* believe it. It explains a lot.' It certainly explained Dickon's dark mood, on occasion. The times when he was sulky, and barely spoke. She thought it was her; that she had done something wrong.

'I don't feel good about it, but if I hadn't helped him out, he'd be in big trouble. He'd probably be sent down. I told him I'd buy it as long as he stopped gambling. He hasn't, though.' Harry shrugged.

'Goodness.' Elspeth tried to take it all in. She remembered Dickon looking out at the sea on the drive down, and the tears in his eyes, and realised it all made sense. He knew what he had lost, and he knew it was his own fault. And that was why he had drunk so much. To forget.

'I don't suppose he'll ever stop,' said Harry. 'People like him don't.'

'What a good friend you are.'

'Am I, though?' said Harry. 'I don't know that it's awfully kind of me to steal his girlfriend.'

He turned and looked into her eyes with his warm gaze.

Elspeth remembered how Dickon never seemed able to remember her name. How he always seemed impatient with her. How he spent most of the day staring at Juliet. How he'd been cross when she'd hurt herself. Even crosser when she was sick.

'I don't think he likes me very much at all. I don't think he'll care.'

There was just the tiniest crescent of sun left.

'So, shall we stay?' Harry asked.

They both turned to look at the beach hut. It looked welcoming in the fading light. A little haven.

On the horizon, the last snippet of sun hovered, as if it wanted to hear her answer before it left for the night.

'Yes,' said Elspeth, thinking she might never get a chance like this again, a chance to fall asleep in Harry's arms with the sound of the waves lulling them, and to wake up next to him, and to watch the sun rise again over the sea.

BIRTHDAY BANQUET
RECIPES

✺

*M*y birthday is in early August, which means very often people are on holiday when it comes to celebrating. But it does also mean the weather is usually fabulous, so I gather together what friends and family I can for a beach banquet. As it's my birthday I don't want to make a load of work for myself, so the answer is an extravagant seafood feast.

For this I go to the harbour, to a little shack on the quayside with tables and chairs outside. Here you can guzzle a *plateau de fruits de mer* with a bottle of white wine and watch the boats meander in and out under the stern gaze of Verity, the die-cast bronze Hirst statue that stands on the end of the pier.

Or you can take your own bountiful seafood platter home with you. We choose the finest specimens and our eyes are inevitably bigger than our stomachs. We stop for bottles of bone-dry Riesling or rich buttery burgundy to wash down our catch.

The vibrant reds and oranges and pinks and corals and creams spread out on a bed of ice is magnificent. It's a ceremonial and celebratory centrepiece, and there is a pleasing ritual to it as well, as claws are cracked open and the sweet flesh pulled from the shells. It's a delicious and messy evening of indulgence, almost decadent, but as it only happens once a year I feel no guilt, only pleasure.

Birthday cocktails

Every good birthday party must start with cocktails, and these are the perfect aperitifs for a summer celebration.

Campari mule

My favourite aperitif is Campari – I love its medicinal sweetness and its incarnadine glow. Campari and soda is my evening go-to, and in winter I love a negroni, but for a summer's evening this cocktail is a little more refreshing and the bubbles make it perfect to kick off a birthday party.

SERVES 1

50ml Campari
15ml elderflower cordial
Juice of 1 lime
Ice
Ginger beer
Mint sprigs

Mix together the Campari, elderflower cordial and lime juice in the bottom of a glass. Add ice and top up with ginger beer. Garnish with a sprig or two of fresh mint.

145

Gin spritz

Campari is a little like Marmite – you either love it or hate it – so for those who are not so keen, this is a gin-based party starter.

SERVES 1

½ cucumber
50ml gin
20ml elderflower cordial
Ice
Soda water
Mint sprigs

Run a vegetable peeler along the cucumber to make thin curls. Drape them around the inside of the glass. Add the gin and elderflower cordial, then the ice, then top up with soda. Garnish with sprigs of fresh mint.

Plateau de fruits de mer with aïoli

A huge plate, smothered in ice, on which is perched a kingly selection of dressed lobster, langoustines and crab, the only accompaniment wedges of bright yellow lemon. And, with it, quivering blobs of garlic aïoli.

SERVES A GREEDY FOURSOME

Selection of fruits de mer

Lemon wedges, to serve

For the aïoli

3 garlic cloves

I tsp sea salt

2 egg yolks

I tsp mustard powder

250ml sunflower oil

I tsp cider vinegar

Crush the garlic with the salt until you have a smooth paste. Plop the egg yolks into the bottom of a bowl and add the garlic paste and mustard and mix together. Add the oil a drop at a time and whisk until you have a thick mixture – take this stage very slowly and have patience. Once it is properly thick you can start to add more oil, in a thin stream, still whisking diligently. When all the oil has been used up, add the vinegar, stirring it in thoroughly. Taste and adjust with more salt and vinegar if needed.

Serve the aïoli with your seafood platter and plenty of lemon to squeeze over.

Potato salad

Like hummus, potato salad is another of those seemingly dull dishes that has a fanatical following. I have had numerous conversations about the best recipe and after much experimentation I think this is the perfect one – delicious in itself but not overpowering, and the best foil for rich seafood. Mayonnaise is too cloying, somehow, so I prefer an oil-based dressing, and serving the potatoes still warm enhances all the flavours.

SERVES 4

650g small new potatoes, washed

3 tbsp extra virgin olive oil

1 tbsp cider vinegar

1 tsp honey

1 tsp Dijon mustard

½ red onion, finely diced

1 tsp capers

Bunch fresh tarragon or dill, finely chopped

Sea salt and freshly ground black pepper

Boil the potatoes in salted water for 10 minutes until they are soft but firm when you poke them with a sharp knife.

Drain and keep warm. Pour the olive oil, vinegar, honey and mustard into a serving bowl and whisk until emulsified. Swish in the red onion, capers and some tarragon or dill. Add the still-warm potatoes and turn them around in the dressing until they are evenly coated. Season with salt and black pepper.

Rosemary and cranberry focaccia

I've always been a little terrified of bread-making and used to buy this focaccia in our little local shop, but they stopped using the concession that supplied it. And then I watched an episode of *Salt Fat Acid Heat* with Samin Nosrat, and became beguiled by the process, my mouth watering at the sight of the golden loaf, rich with olive oil, emerging from the oven. And I asked myself, 'How hard can it be?' Not very, it turns out! And probably the most satisfying thing I've ever done. My first attempt was perfect – the outside crisp, the inside soft and fluffy, just the right amount of salt and herbs. Ideal for mopping up the remains of the aïoli.

MAKES 1 LOAF

500g strong white bread flour, plus extra for dusting

1 × 7g packet yeast

1 tsp olive oil

350ml warm water

1 tsp sea salt, plus extra to scatter over

Handful of dried cranberries

2 rosemary sprigs, leaves stripped

Put the flour and yeast in a large bowl and add the olive oil, water and salt. Stir until the mixture comes together, then remove the dough to a lightly floured surface and knead for a good 5–10 minutes until it becomes smooth and elastic. Pat into a ball and return to the cleaned and oiled bowl, covering it with a clean cloth. Leave it for 1 hour until it has doubled in size. Punch the air out of the dough and then stretch it into a rectangle in an oiled 24 × 30cm baking tin. Leave for another 30–45 minutes.

Preheat the oven to 220°C/fan 200°C/gas mark 7. Add a glug of olive oil to the dough and gently spread over the top, then poke holes in the dough with your index finger or the end of a wooden spoon. Prod a dried cranberry into each hole and sprinkle the rosemary leaves over the top, patting them into the dough a little along with a scattering of sea salt.

Bake the bread for 30 minutes until the top is pale gold. Drizzle another glug of olive oil over the top. Rip apart with your bare hands!

Watermelon, feta and mint salad

This has become my favourite summer salad and it looks stunning too. It's a lovely combination of textures and tastes – sweet, salty and crunchy but also really refreshing. I use a lot of mint in everything during the summer but it really sings here. For ease, I use the pre-cut packets of watermelon you can get in most supermarkets.

500g watermelon flesh
1 × 200g block feta cheese
1 tbsp pumpkin seeds
6 mint sprigs, chopped

Dice the watermelon into bite-size cubes and put in a serving bowl. Chop the feta into smaller cubes and scatter over the watermelon. Toast the pumpkin seeds until they start to pop and scatter over the top together with the fresh mint.

Orange and almond cake

If it's warm, I don't want to take an iced birthday cake down to the beach. And besides, I feel a little old for candles and rousing songs. This cake is the perfect alternative. It is the most glorious saffron-gold, dense, moist, not too sweet and it lasts for ages. I serve it with crème fraîche spiked with Cointreau, orange zest and a little icing sugar.

MAKES 1 CAKE

2 large oranges
250g caster sugar
250g ground almonds
6 large eggs
1 tsp baking powder

Preheat the oven to 220°C/fan 200°C/gas mark 7 and grease and line a 22cm springform tin.

Fill a large pan with water and bring to the boil. Plop the oranges in and cook them for 2 hours. Watch them like a hawk. I have ruined more than one pan by letting it boil dry, so keep topping the water up. You can, if you have a microwave, stick them in there for 10 minutes but then your house won't be filled with a glorious citrussy scent.

Let the oranges cool a little then cut into quarters and remove any pips with a knife. Put them in a food processor and blitz until they are in liquid form.

In a large bowl, beat the sugar, almonds, eggs and baking powder for 2 minutes with a handheld mixer. Then add the pulverised oranges and beat for a further minute. Pour into the tin then bake in the oven for 45–60 minutes, checking after 45 minutes. It is ready when a skewer inserted in the centre comes out quite clean.

A BEACH HUT PARTY
TOP TWENTY

I spent my early teens in America. It was the early seventies, my parents had been posted to Washington DC, and my brother and I felt as if we had stepped into a movie. A fridge that made ice, a telephone mounted on the wall with a long wiggly cord which meant you could wander off for privacy (and no need to wait until after six o'clock for cheap phone calls), air conditioning, a huge car with a brown wooden stripe down the side with a button that wound the windows down automatically … We spent all our summers by the pool at the club we had joined – searingly hot days where you couldn't put your bare feet on the pavement (or the sidewalk!). We made baloney sandwiches with mayo and our tiny transistor radio blared out Lynyrd Skynyrd, Elton John and Led Zeppelin. From those days onwards summer has meant music to me. An aural montage of memories.

Fast-forward on the cassette deck of my life and my eldest son and I sat down to make a beach playlist for this year's birthday. We took it in turns to pick a song that meant summer to us. Of course, this list is personal, bespoke to us and our experiences. But all playlists are unique, pinned to time, place, emotion, the company you are keeping, the person you are in love with …

All these songs have an uplifting vibe to them – the feeling of sun on your skin, a breeze on your face, the scent of the sea.

We will dance on the shore until the fire of the sun dips down below the horizon and the silver moon takes over, lighting up the sands with a pewter glow.

All I Wanna Do – SHERYL CROW

Could You Be Loved – BOB MARLEY

Summer Breeze – THE ISLEY BROTHERS

Smooth – SANTANA

Mr Jones – COUNTING CROWS

Sunday Shining – FINLEY QUAYE

Dani California — RED HOT CHILI PEPPERS

I'm Like a Bird — NELLY FURTADO

Butterfly — CRAZY TOWN

Misirlou — DICK DALE

Good Vibrations — THE BEACH BOYS

What I Am — EDIE BRICKELL & NEW BOHEMIANS

Havana — CAMILA CABELLO

Buck Rogers — FEEDER

Livin' La Vida Loca — RICKY MARTIN

Rock Lobster — THE B-52s

You Don't Love Me (No, No, No) — DAWN PENN

West Coast — LANA DEL REY

Come Away with Me — NORAH JONES

Summertime — ELLA FITZGERALD

Seafood
suppers

Catch of the Day

She couldn't wait. It wasn't often Kim and Jim (people laughed at the way their names rhymed, but what could they do?) went out for dinner. Life was exhausting, especially at this time of year. Winter was harder for Jim, of course, for fishing from November to March was perilous and freezing and thankless. But the summer months were full-on for both of them, for demand was high and the tourists were hungry. Kim was up at dawn, cleaning fish, getting the shop and café ready, buttering bread for crab sandwiches, slicing up lemons, pulling ice out of the freezer … And Jim was out on the trawler, sometimes away for days.

But tonight they had booked dinner at Number 27, the posh restaurant on the quay in Tawcombe. For it was a celebration. Today's catch was going to represent the very last payment on the loan they'd taken out ten years ago, to buy the *Quadrille*.

She could still remember the sick feeling when they'd

signed the paperwork. It had been a terrifying amount of money, but it was Jim's ambition to have his own boat. They'd used the house as collateral. If anything went wrong – if Jim fell ill or was injured, or they had a particularly bad winter, or if the boat was damaged – they would lose the roof over their heads. Their heads and their children's heads – it wasn't just their lives they were putting at risk, but Amy and Noah's too.

But they'd done it. And next week the loan would be paid off and they would be free. Every penny that came in from now on would be theirs. As Kim looked around, she had to admit that they had done something they never dreamed possible. They'd gone from sending the fish to the market along the coast to setting up their own shop on the harbour. Okay, so it wasn't grand. Just an old shipping container with a large counter for laying out the fish. But they'd painted it a rich deep petrol blue and put up a chalkboard to display their prices, and people came in their droves to buy crab sandwiches and pints of prawns and cones of cockles.

And then Kim had pushed for them to open a café area, so Jim had built a platform out of decking so people could sit and eat and watch the boats come and go. And now it was one of the most popular places to eat in Tawcombe, with huge cream umbrellas in case of rain and strings of fairy lights. They were packed out every weekend and pretty much every weeknight too, in the height of the season.

Some people were jealous, of course. Matty Roberts for a start, from the next town along the coast. Matty was their biggest rival. Flashy, successful, ambitious. His wife Natalie looked daggers at Kim when she saw her in the bank. Natalie, who'd never done a day's work since she'd married Matty. And there were women at the school gates who had raised an eyebrow when Kim had bought an old soft-top Audi to whizz around in. It was ancient and limped through its MOT every year, but they seemed to think she was showing off. Kim didn't care what they thought. She had worked her fingers to the bone and if she wanted the roof down and the music up when she drove along the coast road, then that's what she would have and she didn't feel any guilt. You could have whatever you wanted if you worked hard enough, that was her philosophy.

Hard work and risk and teamwork. They couldn't have done it without each other. Jim wouldn't have had the will to go out and battle the elements without Kim to come home to. She was the one who fed him and washed his filthy clothes and warmed him back up in bed. They'd both sat at the kitchen table and done the maths: worked out the repayments, and what would happen if something went wrong, and how long it would be before the house was taken off them if there was a disaster.

And after today, they wouldn't have that hanging over them any more. No one could ever take the house away. The boat was theirs.

Kim's favourite part of the day was laying out the fresh fish on the ice in the counter. It was like a work of art, and the colours were stunning: steel greys and blacks and silvers; cream and coral and orange. There were scallops and mackerel and turbot like flying saucers; salmon and crab; red mullet and sea bass. Brill and John Dory and deep red tuna. And bowls of dark green samphire, too, that tasted of the sea. She loved talking to customers about how they were going to cook their purchases: mostly all that was needed was butter and lemon, but she had her own recipes that she would gladly share: crab linguine, or mussels cooked in local cider, or a luxurious creamy fish pie.

She sold tubs of her own aïoli, too, to eat with lobster. And tartare sauce, to go with fried fish, sharp with capers and cornichons and the aniseed kick of tarragon. And she always had a box of big bright unwaxed lemons which she often threw in for nothing.

She'd gone from being a girl of little confidence to becoming the queen of the harbour. It was Jim who'd brought her out of her shell. She'd been miserable when she met him. She was pulling pints at the pub, having just left school without even taking her exams, convinced she was going to get nowhere, saving up to run off to Bristol. She didn't have the nerve to run to London, and she had cousins who lived on the outskirts of Bristol, so it felt like a safe place to escape to.

Bristol wasn't as safe as Jim, though. Jim was older than her by eight years, but she found that comforting, because he wasn't a show-off. Wasn't going to drive her too fast in his car or sell her dodgy pills or get off with someone else behind her back, like the other boys in Tawcombe. He was kind, thoughtful, steadfast. By that Christmas, they were married, and everyone said it would never last, she was too young, at only just seventeen.

They'd certainly proved them wrong. Kim smiled as she arranged a dozen dressed crabs, the white and brown meat neatly divided inside the pale-pink shells. Two kids, a bright and sunny bungalow on the outskirts of Tawcombe with a sea view, the boat, the shop and café – and as from this week they would be debt-free. It had taken them over twenty years, but it proved she had been right to let the man with the bright blue eyes buy her a drink that evening. She still loved him, those eyes still sparkling in his weathered skin, his beard growing through white now. And his hair. She clippered that for him in the kitchen every two weeks, close to his head. He looked good.

Her first customers of the day were hovering by the counter and she looked up to smile at them.

'Let me know if you need any help,' she said. She was never pushy. She didn't need to be. People often became overexcited and got carried away, ordering more than they could possibly eat. They were on holiday, and wanted to spoil themselves, so they did. She loved watching their faces and listening while they debated what to choose. She would hand over the bags, groaning with the day's catch, and they wouldn't find fresher anywhere.

'What do you recommend?' It was a woman, probably in her early fifties, with a much younger man. Kim eyed them curiously, wondering about their relationship. The woman was a bit older than Kim but very glamorous, with huge sunglasses and a turquoise beaded kaftan, her hands flashing with diamonds. Her companion was rock-star skinny in his faded jeans and Ray-Bans. They both looked as if they *were* somebody. Yet there was a politeness between them that suggested they didn't know each other all that well. She was asking him what his favourite shellfish was – not his mum then, though she was certainly old enough to be.

Then Kim looked closer and realised who the woman was, and her heart leapt with excitement. They often had celebrities down on the harbour. It was a popular weekend destination for a quick holiday. She'd seen soap stars and footballers and, of course, the occasional TV chef who would engage in conversation. She was never starstruck, but this woman was different.

Caroline Talbot. Kim had every single one of her books. Jim bought them for her in hardback, every Christmas, and they were her absolute guilty pleasure. She was lost in another world for the time it took to read them. She had them all lined up in a row on a shelf in the front room, in order. She knew everything there was to know about Tuesday DeVille.

Would it be wrong, to be a total fangirl? Caroline was pointing at a magnificent turbot in the centre of the counter – the king of the display.

'How would I cook this?'

'You're best to cook it whole, bone in,' Kim told her, her mouth dry with nerves. 'In the oven, with some olive oil and lemon juice. About half an hour.'

'What do you think?' Caroline looked at the boy – man? – with her. 'Do you like turbot?'

'I dunno. Where I come from, fish comes in batter. From the chippy.' He grinned at Kim, who had the strange feeling she knew him, but of course she couldn't possibly. There was no one like him in Tawcombe.

'You just need some new potatoes and a bit of salad,' she told them. 'Beautiful. You won't get fresher than him.'

'We'll have it,' said Caroline.

Kim lifted the turbot ceremoniously and wrapped it carefully in brown paper. She hesitated, nervous, but decided to go for it. How often did you get to meet one of your heroes?

'Can I just say ... I absolutely love your books,' she said to Caroline as she handed it over. 'My husband's a fisherman and I sometimes can't sleep when it's rough out there for worrying about him. Your books take my mind off it.'

Caroline's face lit up. 'Oh,' she said. 'That's lovely to hear. I'm down here writing at the moment. I shall think of you when I get stuck.'

'I hope you don't mind me mentioning it.'

'No writer ever minds,' Caroline assured her. She turned to her companion. 'Do we, Radar?'

He shook his head, laughing. 'We love praise. It's what we live for.'

'Oh,' said Kim, the penny dropping. She'd seen pictures of him in the paper, and in magazines at the hairdresser. 'Are you … Radar Thingy?'

'Yeah. For my sins.'

'My daughter never reads usually but she loved your book.' Amy and her friends had sighed over his photo.

'Well, hopefully there's another one on the way.' He nodded his head towards Caroline. 'She's got me locked up. I'm only allowed out for an hour at dinner time. She'll chain me up again till tea.'

'Don't listen to him,' said Caroline, handing over her credit card.

Kim looked at them both. Wondering. Were they an item? They certainly seemed happy together.

'Well, good luck with the writing. And enjoy your fish.'

She watched them leave the harbour, Caroline sweeping along in her kaftan, Radar strolling beside her like her consort. Good on her, Kim thought, if they did have something going on.

The encounter had made what was already a good day into an even better one, and she looked forward to telling Jim about it over dinner. Neither of them usually had anything out of the ordinary to talk about. Bits of town gossip and the kids was their usual topic of conversation. She liked it like that, to be honest. It was safe, familiar territory.

'Hey, look at you,' she said later that evening as Jim came into the kitchen ready to go out. He had on the dark blue floral shirt she'd bought him for his birthday, and it made his eyes seem even brighter. He hadn't been sure about the flowers, but there was something about his hard muscles under the soft fabric that made Kim still melt.

She'd put on a dress, a change from her usual sweatshirt and jeans, and had her hair in mermaid waves, like Amy had taught her, instead of scraped back in a ponytail.

'We scrub up okay, don't we?' she laughed, taking his arm for the walk into town.

At the restaurant, they ordered a bottle of prosecco to celebrate their last payment and their first night out for months. Kim raised her glass, her eyes shining.

'Well, here's to being debt-free.' She frowned when Jim hesitated to touch his glass to hers. 'What is it?'

'There's something I need to tell you.'

Oh God. He was ill. With what? Or he was going to leave her. Who for? She raked her mind for possible diseases, possible temptresses. 'What is it?'

'Jed Matthews is packing it in. He's giving me first refusal on the *Pelican*.'

Jed Matthews was the oldest fisherman in Tawcombe. He'd taught Jim everything he knew. The *Pelican* was the most envied boat in the harbour. State of the art.

'Well, you can do just that. Refuse.' Kim smiled, thinking that was that. Then she frowned. Jim was staring at her.

'It's a great opportunity, Kim. She's a lovely boat. I know every inch of her. He'd give me a good price.'

'We'd have to take out another loan. We'd have to pay another crew.' Kim could feel panic rising inside her. The relief of being debt-free had been massive. The thought of taking on another loan made her feel sick.

'It's the perfect way to grow the business. And Noah …' He looked down at the table. 'Noah's been talking to me. He wants to join me.'

Kim could feel herself crumple.

'I thought he wanted to go to uni. I thought he wanted to do marine studies.'

'He doesn't see the point in spending three years studying and getting into debt. He wants to earn money, Kim. He wants to be independent. Start living his life.'

It was a fair argument. She could see that. But she didn't want Noah out at sea with his dad. She couldn't manage both of them out there full-time. The fear. The worry. The sleepless nights. She thought of the books, the Caroline

Talbot books that had kept her from going completely mad.

'I don't think I can handle that,' she said, her voice very small. She didn't want to hold them back or stamp on their ambitions. But as a wife and mother, it was too much to bear. She knew they didn't understand. She knew they thought they were invincible. You had to, or you'd never go out.

'I won't do it without your blessing,' Jim said. 'But Matty Roberts will buy the *Pelican* if I don't, and Noah says he'll join him.'

Oh no. Anyone but Matty. Kim knew Matty would be glad to have Noah, a local lad brought up on the sea who knew what he was doing. Her stomach roiled like the water in the harbour when a storm was brewing. She took another sip of prosecco but it burned. She wanted to cry. This was supposed to be a joyful celebration.

A tear trickled out onto her cheek. She let it fall unchecked. Let Jim see her cry. She never cried.

He reached out and brushed it away. 'Kim. If we just stop here, and don't push ourselves, what are we going to do with our lives? We've got another twenty years of work left in us. We should be investing. We didn't notice that mortgage payment in the end. If we don't put that money towards growing the business, it'll just get frittered away. We owe it to the kids, to show them how to better yourself.'

'We have bettered ourselves! We started out with nothing.'

'But we could have more. And they could have more. It is all for them, in the end.'

Kim stared at him. She was angry now. 'So you've made up your mind? Is that what you're saying?'

Jim put down his glass. 'This wasn't my plan,' he said firmly. 'But Jed offering me the *Pelican* did get me thinking. It's too good an opportunity. If we don't grab it, someone else will have her. That's fish we could be selling. Profit we could be making. And if we put a good team together, that's Noah's future sorted.'

'I wanted more for him.' Kim looked at her husband.

'More?' Jim looked blank. 'This is as good as it gets, Kim. Our way of life. On our terms. In our home town. Surrounded by people who know and love us. Why wouldn't you want that for Noah?'

'I wanted him to have an adventure. Do all the things we've never done. What have we ever done?' She put her glass down. 'I've never even been to London, Jim.'

'You could have been. You know that. There's nothing stopping him doing all of those things if he wants to. He can travel the world when he takes time off. He'll have money. He'll be different from us.'

She put her face in her hands. She couldn't think. She tried to make sense of everything Jim was saying. And the trouble was, she knew he was right. She'd seen Noah on the boat, confident and at home. He knew the ropes. He'd be a good fisherman. And Jim was right about them not standing still. It would be too easy to coast along now the debt was paid off. She knew she worked harder when she was under pressure, and thought of ways to bring in more cash. You had to be hungry to get on.

And she wasn't going to let Matty Roberts get his hands on her boy. Wasn't going to let Matty's wife Natalie flash her a triumphant smile when she bumped into her. Natalie with her long red nails and hair extensions. She was not going to let Noah pay for Natalie's life of luxury.

She sat quietly while the waiter refilled their glasses. This was how life worked. It set you challenges. It changed course. It made you think differently, about yourself and those around you. And it was a compromise. Things didn't always go the way you wanted them to. When that happened, you had to adapt. This hadn't been her dream for Noah, but she would get used to it. They would make it a success. They were a team.

And perhaps she'd feel a sense of pride, not fear, when she looked out into the harbour and saw them chugging out to sea. And she'd still have her boy nearby. He'd buy a little house in the town. Marry a lovely girl. She'd look after the grandkids, eventually. Not everyone had that.

She picked up her glass again. She felt calm and composed. And proud. Jim and Noah would be a great partnership. She didn't know where Amy would fit in yet.

Amy, who wanted to study theatrical make-up at college and get as far away from Tawcombe as she could. She'd be behind her, whatever she decided. That's what you did, as a mum.

She held her glass out to Jim.

'To the *Pelican*,' she said, and as he took in her words his eyes crinkled up with pleasure. She didn't know anyone with bluer eyes.

'To the *Pelican*,' he echoed, and she felt the bond between them tighten, as strong as a fisherman's knot.

SEAFOOD SUPPER
RECIPES

✺

I am so lucky where I live to have access to freshly caught fish. As well as the fishmonger on the harbour, there is a fish van that comes on a Thursday with a tempting display nestling on ice – bright eyes look out at me, silver skin glitters in the sunlight, offset by the coral-pink of prawns and scallops and slabs of salmon. The scent of ozone makes my mouth water and choosing is almost impossible, and it's usually my wallet that dictates my purchases.

It took a while for me to be confident enough to experiment with everything on offer and not just plump for the familiar. This summer, I bought an enormous brill, as big as a car tyre, and under the guidance of my chef friend Simon Browne was able to fillet it, with a sharp knife and a sharp eye. We ate the fillets cooked in butter, with a fennel, orange and watercress salad and tiny cubes of roasted potato (the perfect accompaniment to any plain fish), and I felt a huge sense of achievement.

It's a great outing, when we have guests, to go to the fishmonger on the harbour and choose our catch. Whether it's just a bag of prawns to pull apart and eat with granary bread and butter, or a dozen celebratory oysters to put on a silver tray, there's always a sense of ceremony and excitement.

Often nothing much needs to be done – the fish speaks for itself. But here are a few of our family favourites.

Fish pie

I like to keep fish pie simple. Others like to add spinach, broccoli, sweetcorn, mushrooms or halved eggs, but I prefer just adding some parsley to the sauce, and then serving a selection of lovely crisp green vegetables on the side: green beans, mangetout or sugar snap peas, or a mound of good old Birds Eye peas!

Mashed potato or pastry for the top is a matter of personal preference too. Mash makes it more of a nursery dish and slightly more comforting, while pastry provides a crunchy contrast.

I quite often divide the mix and the topping into four individual dishes, which is useful if people are wandering in at different times to be fed. In which case, they only need 20 minutes in the oven.

SERVES 4

800g mixed fish, cut into 2cm chunks – I use a mix
of salmon, cod and smoked haddock

Sea salt and freshly ground black pepper

500ml semi-skimmed milk

50g butter

1 tbsp flour

1 tbsp finely chopped parsley

Juice of ½ lemon

1 tbsp crème fraîche

200g raw king prawns, shells removed

For a mash topping

1kg floury potatoes, peeled

50g butter

1 tbsp milk

Handful of grated Cheddar cheese (optional)

For a pastry topping

1 × 320g sheet ready-rolled puff pastry

Preheat the oven to 220°C/fan 200°C/gas mark 7.

If using the potatoes as a topping, boil them in salted water until tender. Drain thoroughly and put through a potato ricer, then add the butter and milk and beat until you have a lovely smooth buttery mash.

Put the fish in an ovenproof dish, season and cover with the milk. Put in the oven for 10 minutes to gently poach. Remove from the oven, strain the milk into a pan and set aside the fish. Put the milk over a low heat and add the butter and flour. Whisk gently while the butter melts and the flour is incorporated. Bring to the boil then turn down the heat and simmer for a few minutes, whisking all the time until the sauce starts to thicken. Cook for about 5 minutes, then add the parsley, lemon juice and crème fraîche, stirring until it's all nicely mixed in. Add the prawns and heat through until they turn pink, then gently stir in the cooked fish.

Put the fish mixture back into the ovenproof dish, smooth out and then top with either the mashed potato or the flaky pastry. You can, if you like, sprinkle some grated Cheddar over the potato, but I find this a flavour too many and prefer the mash plain against the fish.

Put in the oven for 30 minutes until the potato is browned on top or the pastry is golden.

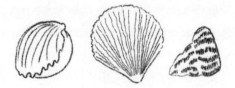

Lobster mac and cheese

This seriously luxurious comfort-food classic is a real indulgence if you have guests. I sometimes serve it in individual copper dishes for the ultimate wow-factor. Bringing it to the table with its golden crust bubbling away always means groans of anticipation. Nursery food with a grown-up edge.

SERVES 4

2 cooked lobsters (you need about 1kg meat)
400g dried macaroni

For the sauce

1 tbsp butter
1 white onion, finely chopped
1 tbsp flour
125ml dry white wine
400ml full-fat milk
2 tsp Dijon mustard
200g Gruyère or Comté cheese, grated
Sea salt and freshly ground black pepper

For the breadcrumb topping

1 tbsp butter
1 garlic clove, finely chopped
100g breadcrumbs
Handful of flat-leaf parsley, finely chopped
100g Gruyère cheese, grated

Preheat the oven to 220°C/fan 200°C/gas mark 7.

Using a large sharp knife, cut lengthways through the head of the lobster, down the body and through the tail to give you two halves. Discard the head, gills and any pink roe and remove the pinky-white meat from the tail. Crack the pincers with a nutcracker and remove the meat with a skewer. If you have the patience, crack the legs and use a skewer to prise out the meat. Cut the lobster meat into even chunks.

Cook the macaroni in boiling water according to the packet instructions, until al dente. Drain and set aside.

To make the sauce, melt the butter in a saucepan, add the onion and sweat until nicely soft. Add the flour and cook gently for a minute or so, then add the wine and whisk to remove any lumps. Add the milk a little at a time, continuing to whisk, then cook over a low heat for 5 minutes until the sauce is slightly thickened. Add the mustard and cheese and stir until it's melted. Season well.

For the breadcrumb topping, melt the butter in a frying pan and add the garlic, taking care not to burn. Tip in the breadcrumbs and coat evenly in the garlicky butter. Remove from the heat and stir in the parsley and cheese.

Stir the sauce into the macaroni then add the lobster. Pour into an ovenproof dish and add the breadcrumb topping. Transfer to the oven and cook for 15 minutes until bubbling and the topping is nicely browned.

Crab linguine

This is one hundred per cent our family favourite. It's super-quick to prepare – you will barely have finished your first glass of wine before it is ready. I buy two dressed crabs to make this, stirring the brown meat through first to coat the linguine, then scattering the sweeter, lighter white meat on afterwards, though it doesn't really matter if it all gets mixed together in the process.

SERVES 4

1 × 500g packet dried linguine

1 tbsp olive oil

2 garlic cloves, finely chopped

1 red chilli, deseeded and finely chopped

2 dressed crabs, about 120g each

Zest and juice of 1 lemon

Sea salt and freshly ground black pepper

Handful of chopped flat-leaf parsley

Bring a large pan of salted water to the boil and cook the linguine according to the packet instructions, until al dente. Remove from the heat and drain, reserving about 50ml of the cooking water for the sauce and returning the linguine to the saucepan.

In a small frying pan, heat the oil gently and add the garlic and chilli. Cook gently for a couple of minutes, taking care not to burn.

Add the brown crab meat to the frying pan and stir to warm through. Add most of the lemon zest (keep some to garnish) and the juice and season to taste. Stir this mixture through the drained linguine in the saucepan and warm through. If it feels a little dry, which it can do, add some more olive oil or the reserved pasta cooking water to loosen it a little. Then scatter the white crab meat, parsley and reserved lemon zest over the top, and serve.

Vodka prawn penne

Adding vodka to a home-made tomato sauce is one of my favourite discoveries: there's something about its addition that makes the tomato sweeter and less acidic and unlocks even more flavour. Happily the combination lends itself well to the addition of prawns, so this is a really stylish and robust pasta dish that should put a smile on everyone's face.

SERVES 4

400g dried penne
50g butter
2 garlic cloves, crushed
4 large vine tomatoes, finely chopped
400g frozen raw king prawns
Sea salt and freshly ground black pepper
50ml vodka
Zest and juice of 1 lemon
100g crème fraîche
Handful of chopped flat-leaf parsley

Cook the penne in a large pan of boiling salted water according to the packet instructions, until al dente.

Meanwhile, in a wide saucepan, melt the butter and add the garlic, taking care not to burn. Tip in the tomatoes and cook for 5 minutes until softened, then add the frozen prawns, season and stir everything together. Keeping over a low heat, add the vodka and lemon zest and juice. Heat through gently until the prawns have all turned pink. Stir in the crème fraîche and warm through.

Drain the penne and tip into the sauce, stirring until it is evenly distributed and making sure everything has warmed through. Scatter over the parsley.

Paella

Spanish paella is a hearty and sociable dish. This version is far from authentic, but it is quick and easy and flavoursome and perfect for bringing to the table with a fanfare!

SERVES 4

8 skin-on, bone-in chicken thighs

1 tsp hot smoked paprika

Sea salt

1 lemon, cut into 8 wedges

Olive oil

50g butter

1 onion, thinly sliced

1 garlic clove, crushed

50g chorizo, thinly sliced

1 red pepper, thinly sliced

400g paella rice

1 litre hot chicken stock

2 saffron strands

1 × 300g packet frozen mixed seafood
(mussels, squid, prawns), raw but defrosted

150g frozen peas

8 large crevettes, cooked

Handful of chopped flat-leaf parsley

Preheat the oven to 220°C/fan 200°C/gas mark 7.

Rub the chicken thighs with the paprika, put into an ovenproof dish and sprinkle with some sea salt. Squeeze 2 lemon wedges over the chicken and tuck the rest among the thighs. Drizzle with some olive oil and put in the oven until cooked through and the juices run clear – about 25 minutes. Keep warm in a low oven.

While the chicken is cooking, melt the butter in a large flat-bottomed pan. I have a paella pan, but I sometimes use my flat-bottomed wok if I'm not making a huge paella. Add the onion, garlic, chorizo and red pepper, and cook gently until softened, about 10 minutes. Tip in the paella rice and stir until coated, then cook for a couple of minutes while you mix the chicken stock with the saffron. Pour the stock over the rice, bring to the boil and turn down the heat to very low, leaving the rice to absorb the stock. This will take about 15 minutes.

Towards the end, stir through the seafood and peas and heat through until thoroughly cooked. Top with the chicken thighs, then garnish with the crevettes and the chopped parsley.

West Country mussels

We are lucky where we live to have an abundant choice of West Country cider, and I use it a lot in cooking: the apple-y tartness cuts through so perfectly in both sweet and savoury dishes. It's ideal for mussels – I love lugging a big net home, and the clatter as I tip them into the sink to wash. Less than fifteen minutes later I can bring a huge pot to the table for everyone to share, the empty shells piling up as everyone slurps their way through. And the scent as they are cooking just smells of holiday.

SERVES 4

2kg net of mussels
50g butter
1 large onion, chopped
2 garlic cloves, chopped
125ml cider
1 tbsp chopped flat-leaf parsley
2 tbsp crème fraîche
Sea salt and freshly ground black pepper

Rinse the mussels in cold water, pull off any beards and make sure they are all closed. Give any that aren't closed a sharp

tap to see if that will make them shut. Discard any that are still open. In a large lidded pan, melt the butter and sweat the onion for 10 minutes until nice and soft, then add the garlic and cook for 1 minute. Add the cider and let it bubble away for a few minutes. Tip in the *moules*, mix them around then cover and steam for about 5 minutes. Shake the pan from time to time. After 5 minutes take a look to see if the mussels are mostly open. If not, give them a couple more minutes.

Drain the mussels into a colander, keeping the cidery liquid. Discard any mussels that are still closed. Put a lid on the mussels to keep them warm. Pour the liquid back into the pan, add half the parsley and boil for a couple of minutes to reduce, then add the crème fraîche. Season to taste.

Serve the mussels in a big bowl and pour over the cider sauce. Sprinkle over the rest of the parsley.

Family
favourites

Behind the Façade

As Reg lay back in the stripy deckchair staring at the shore, his arms folded behind his head, he thought it was probably the first time he had relaxed for years. He couldn't get used to the feeling. It was a sensation he usually only got after several beers, but this wasn't as fuzzy; he could still notice things. Beer was anaesthetising, while right now he felt fully alert, able to enjoy his surroundings. He wasn't even going to let what had happened get to him. He was one hundred per cent chilled. One hundred per cent.

He wasn't quite sure what he put it down to. It couldn't just be because Lily wasn't there. That wasn't fair. Maybe it was because the kids were that bit older? He didn't have to hover over them quite so much. They were nine and seven, and although he still had them in his eyeline, he could let them think they were doing their own thing. It was important to give children a sense of independence.

Or maybe it was the setting? He'd landed with his bum

in the honey, he had to admit. His clients were often grateful and gave him thank-you gifts, but this was the most generous gesture of appreciation yet: a whole week by the sea in a beach hut.

'It's sitting empty until August, when all the family go down,' his client had told him. 'My husband won't let me rent it out, but I know he'd be delighted to let you use it. It would be our pleasure. You've done a fantastic job on the bathroom. No stress at all.'

That's what happened when you went the extra mile. People were good to you. Reg never left a job until he was completely sure the client was happy, and it paid off. A lot of his mates got the job done as quickly as they could and sent off the invoice, but in Reg's view that was a false economy. And this was the proof. He'd re-grouted Felicity Banner's bathroom three times before she was satisfied. Every other plumber he knew would have told her to stick her grout where the sun didn't shine after the second attempt. His patience had been rewarded.

The beach hut was like something out of another age. The England not of his youth, but his grandfather's. Deck-chairs. Windbreaks. Rock pools. Sandcastles. Ninety-nine ice creams. Sand between your toes. Simple pleasures. It made up for the awfulness of the situation.

He didn't want to think about the row he and Lily had. If he wasn't careful he would start feeling guilty, but he'd had to stand his ground. The situation had got out of control. He didn't know what was going to happen next, but, in the meantime, he was going to make things as normal as he could for the children. Well, except for the fact that he'd banned anything electrical, as there was no wi-fi in the beach hut. There had been protests at first, but it was amazing how quickly they'd forgotten to plug themselves in.

The two of them were totally engrossed with putting the finishing touches to the sandcastle he'd built with them. He'd shown them how to do it properly, something he remembered from his own childhood and somehow not forgotten. It was engrained in him, the science of mixing sand and water in the right proportions, of building solid foundations. And the result was a magnificent sprawling castle that any king would be proud of. Elsie and Zak were smoothing the walls into shape, widening the moat, pressing shells onto the walls and sticking the little paper flags he'd bought onto the ramparts. He couldn't remember the last time they'd played together like this.

He looked at his watch. He should probably start cooking. The kids would be starving – the sea air had given them appetites he could hardly keep up with. He was looking forward to making them dinner. He loved cooking. He'd always fancied himself as a bit of a chef. He loved messing about in the kitchen, doing his Jamie Oliver impersonation which always made them laugh. He'd do something simple they could stick on a plate and take outside to eat with their fingers. Tacos. Or chicken souvlaki. Something spicy. Pukka!

And thank God there would be no bloody performance before they got stuck into their food for once. The whole thing had taken over their life. From the minute they got out of bed, Lily was there with her phone, directing every single moment, making sure they looked like the perfect family. Nothing on her timeline remotely reflected the reality of their everyday life. Every item of clothing was picked out for them, every hair on their head was either smoothed or ruffled, depending on the mood she was going for. Everything around them was positioned carefully. Even the dog wasn't allowed to be itself. Everything was themed, and colour co-ordinated, and styled, and curated, into a life that Reg didn't recognise as their own.

And Reg was rarely allowed in shot. A big burly plumber with a beard and a bit of a tummy? He didn't suit the narrative at all. He was a lovely bloke but he wasn't photogenic. He laughed it off, but of course he was hurt. No one likes being left out. He'd put up with it to start with, because the whole 'influencer' thing seemed to have given Lily back the confidence she'd lost and, anyway, it was his fault. When she was made redundant from the recruitment company she'd worked for, he suggested it as a joke.

'Why don't you set yourself up as an influencer? You've got a good eye.'

And she did. She was always moving things around in the house, changing the colour scheme, styling it up to look fresh, and their friends were always amazed by her ingenuity in making things look a million dollars despite only spending pennies. She had an eye for a bargain and was the queen of the discount stores. And there was nothing she didn't know about upcycling. He often came home to find a familiar piece of furniture had been sanded down, repainted and given a crackle glaze or, worse, a layer of decoupage.

Within a month, she had a thousand followers. Within six months, ten thousand. And it grew from there.

He'd started to object when he could see how it was affecting the kids. They spent their whole life posing, Elsie with one hip jutting out and a bit of a pout, while Zak had a variety of slouchy poses with his hands in his pockets or his back against the wall with one leg up behind him. They had, Reg learned later, had several online tutorials teaching them how to stand. They were mannequins being remotely controlled by their own mother. But they could no longer behave like normal children. Of course, they were all over it when some new toy or gadget or appliance arrived, ripping open the box with gleeful frenzy. But he thought what they really wanted was a stable home and a mum who could pay them attention for more than five minutes. It wasn't as if he wasn't working hard enough to give them everything they needed.

'I don't think it's good for them,' Reg told Lily. 'I think you should stop for a bit. Think about doing something else. I mean, it can't last forever, can it?'

'But this is so easy!' Lily protested. 'I can do it without even leaving the house. Without even getting out of bed! This is how we get all that stuff, Reg. I don't see you turning your nose up at it. Our life is so much better for it. If we want something, I figure out how we can get it for free, and then it arrives on the doorstep.'

This was true. She had hundreds of thousands of followers. She was great at telling the kind of visual lies people seemed to want to lap up. Every waking moment was spent thinking about the next set-up. And she was high on her own success. But she was wrong. It wasn't easy. It was hell. They weren't allowed to relax for a second, any of them. And behind the façade their life was chaos. Everything in frame was perfect, but out of shot there were piles of props, clothes, boxes, clutter and mess that Lily didn't seem able to see. She never had time to restore their life so it matched the lies. Reg did his best to reimpose order but he often didn't get home till gone seven. And he didn't like to point out that he was the one earning the actual money. Lily's freebies were the icing on the cake, but they didn't pay the mortgage.

And she was never off her phone. She was constantly counting the likes on her latest post, and responding to her followers with inane, gushing comments. It was impossible to have a conversation with her unless she started it, in which case you probably had two minutes before she was distracted again.

Every day the delivery man staggered up the path with boxes: scented candles that smelled like toilet cleaner; fondue sets; glittery fake eyelashes; electrical appliances that smoothed or curled your hair. Kitchen gadgets that were totally unnecessary – why did you need a popcorn maker when you could make it in a saucepan with a lid on? And the packaging drove Reg nuts. He spent every evening folding down cardboard boxes for the recycling bin.

Occasionally it would be something worth having. The day they were given a flashy SUV to drive round in for twenty-four hours had been fun. They cruised around fiddling with all the extras and the kids watched movies in the back seat from screens embedded in the head rests. But it just left them with the feeling that their own car was lacking once it was sent back.

It was hollow. Shallow. But Lily couldn't see it. She was hell-bent on world domination, trying to grab the biggest prizes. And when she was offered a week in Ibiza at a new resort, Reg put his foot down.

'I want a proper family holiday. I want to relax. I don't want to be on show. I don't want to have to stop what I'm doing every five minutes and take a picture. And nor do the kids.'

'Fine,' said Lily, her eyes flashing with fury. 'I'll go on my own, then. It's me they want. I'm the one with influence.'

Reggie stared at her. How had she become such a monster? His sweet, funny, kind Lily. But what could he do? He wasn't a controlling man, who wanted to be in charge of his wife's career or what she did every day. Far from it. He wanted her to be fulfilled. He wanted her to have ambition. He wanted her to be a success.

But not at the cost of their family. Not at the cost of Lily herself. He wanted his old Lily back. His comrade. His partner in crime. His friend and his lover. She'd lost her softness and her humour. She'd become hard and brittle and driven.

He'd taken her to the airport yesterday. Of course he had. He wasn't about to stop her going on the holiday of her dreams, and he'd got the beach hut lined up for him and the kids. She and all the other influencers were staying at the swishest airport hotel as the flight was so early the next morning. She'd taken a photo as they left the house, of her surrounded by her luggage (gifted) and her cashmere yoga pants and hoodie for travelling (gifted) and her outsize sunglasses (gifted) and posted it: *Sooooo excited to be off to Ibiza's newest Dream Resort #holiday #dreamcometrue #blessed #watchthisspace.*

She didn't have to give anything a second thought. Reg had it all covered, because their parenting had always been about teamwork. He did his share, straight down the middle, because his own mum and dad had taught him that was what you did. You divided all the graft between you, and if you were better at something than the other person, that was your domain. Lily was better at hedge-cutting than him, because she was meticulous about straight lines, and he was better at making beds, tucking everything as tight as it could be. So they played to their strengths.

But lately, he felt like the hired help. He didn't mind housework or childcare or any of it, but she just assumed he'd pick up the slack. And he was knackered. The last thing he wanted was to become a nag, or spend his time moaning, so he held his tongue. Maybe this week was what they needed? A break from it all. And each other. He and the kids could chill out and relax and do exactly what they wanted without being choreographed. And she could control every moment of her trip to Ibiza, every outfit, every cocktail, every sunset shot.

He'd talk to her when she got back. See if they could find a way of going back to their old selves, without sacrificing her achievement or cramping her style. Perhaps a ban on photos at the weekends? It was the relentlessness of it he couldn't cope with. He stood up with a sigh, checked that both of the kids were still in sight, and headed into the hut to think about food.

He stopped in his tracks. She was there, standing on the

doorstep. In the same outfit he'd left her in the day before, but not looking so groomed and sleek. She had no make-up on, and her hair was scraped back into a scrunchie.

'Lily?' He rushed towards her. 'What's happened?'

'I didn't get on the plane.' Her face crumpled. 'I got the train down here.'

'Why?'

'They were awful. All the other people who were going. They completely ignored me. They all knew each other, and they just acted as if I wasn't there. They were so up themselves. I felt like a nobody.'

He didn't like to ask her what on earth she'd expected. He could have told her what she would be walking into. But he wouldn't take pleasure in saying, 'I told you so.' She looked so fragile and shaken and vulnerable. She'd been living in a make-believe world, and had gone crashing into the hard truth. He was there for her. They were there for her. Her family.

He put his arms around her and pulled her to him. She felt tiny in his arms, and he squeezed her tight.

'Mum!' Elsie and Zak had spotted her and come racing up, their faces alive with excitement to see her. 'What are you doing here?'

'Hey, you guys. Change of plan.' She held out her arms and they ran into them. 'What have you been doing?'

'We made a sandcastle. And we've been rock-pooling. Can we take you to the rock pools?'

'Sure!' She looked at Reg for approval and he nodded.

'They're just over there. We've got half an hour before the tide comes in. Let's do it.'

'Great.' She started to gather her things together, reaching in her bag. He could see it – the wild-eyed twitch of an addict as she assessed the situation and how she could feed her habit. What did she need to make the perfect pose? What should the kids be wearing, holding? What props did they need?

'Lily,' said Reg gently.

She took in a deep breath and nodded. She was clutching her phone to her chest. With a supreme effort of will, she tucked it into her pocket. 'Okay,' she whispered.

She followed them to the top of the beach where the rock pools were. The tide had again gone out so the rocks were revealed, black and gleaming, studded with shiny barnacles and bright green moss. And between them the pools were brimming, teeming with sea life: tiny crabs and anemones and little creatures that shot away before you could identify them. The late afternoon sun was mellow and gentle, bathing them all in a warm glow.

'They've got freckles already,' smiled Lily, looking at the kids leaping over the rocks.

'I know. And I smothered them in Factor 50,' said Reg.

They looked like different children. Their hair was wild, soaked in salt from the sea, sticking out at all angles. Their clothes were covered in sand; their hands and faces grubby.

They were wielding the shrimping nets and buckets they'd bought earlier, peering into the crevasses and corners of every pool. Totally absorbed.

'They look beautiful.' Lily had tears in her eyes.

'Hey.' Reg reached out an arm and pulled her in.

'I've been such a fool,' she said. 'I didn't realise how much it was taking over our lives.'

'Listen,' he said. 'You were doing it for us. You got carried away. It's not your fault you struck gold. But the trick is knowing when to stop. Not get greedy.'

'I thought I could have anything I wanted. I didn't realise I already had everything I needed.'

'We're still here.'

'But you might not have been. I could see it in your eyes, when we had that row. I thought you might leave me. I was so up myself I didn't care. I thought I didn't need you. But I do.'

'I need you too, Lily.' Reg picked up her hand and squeezed it. 'But I want the real you. The old you.'

'What will I do, though?'

'There's loads of things you can do. You're amazing.'

'*You're* amazing. I couldn't have done it without you holding it all together.'

'Well, okay, yeah. Let's agree how amazing I am.' He grinned at her.

'There's one thing I'm going to do.'

'What?'

She pulled her phone out of her pocket and, before he could stop her, she dropped it into the rock pool. It lay in the bottom, lime-green fronds of sea moss drifting gently around it.

'Lily!' Reg looked aghast. 'You can't leave it in there.'

He reached down to fish it out but Lily grabbed his arm.

'No. Leave it in there long enough for it to do some real damage.'

They both sat staring at the blank screen as Zak raced over with a bucket and held it out for them to inspect.

'Look at all the little crabs!'

Lily looked down into the bucket. 'Wow!'

'Aren't you going to take a picture?' Her son looked at her, his little face puzzled.

'No,' she said. 'I'm not taking any more pictures.'

Zak looked suspicious. 'Ooooh-kaaaaay,' he said. 'Weird.'

Reg and Lily burst out laughing. Elsie came running up, her hair flying. 'What's so funny?'

'Mum's being weird,' Zak told her. Then he saw the phone at the bottom of the pool. 'Mum. Your phone!' He went to grab it. 'It's okay. I'll put it in a bag of rice. Dad, we have rice, right?'

'It doesn't matter,' said Lily. 'I don't need it any more.'

'Did you get a new one? Does that mean I can have your old one?'

'I want it!' Elsie was indignant.

Reg took the phone off Zak. 'I think it's beyond repair. And you haven't got long before the tide comes in. Go and see what else you can find. We'll go and have something to eat in a minute.'

The two of them raced off again. Lily sighed. 'They're having a wonderful time.'

'It's pretty special here. And we've done a lot. It's paradise.'

'The beach hut looks cool.'

'It's a home from home. You fall asleep to the sound of the waves. And the stars! Wait until you see the stars.'

Lily put her head on his shoulder. 'Who needs Ibiza?'

'Well, not us. I mean, we had our Ibiza days. The kids will have their Ibiza days, eventually. But right now this is perfect.' He slipped his hand into hers. His heart felt so much lighter. He felt so relieved she had come to her senses, without the whole thing becoming an issue between them. He'd support her in whatever she wanted to do next. They would be a normal family again.

Afterwards, they wandered back up to the beach hut, and Reg went inside to make dinner while Elsie and Zak insisted on burying Lily up to her neck. She seemed quite happy to be their victim, laughing as spadefuls of damp sand were thrown over her and they patted it down carefully around her until she was like a mummy in a sarcophagus.

Reg brought out black bean chilli and tacos and bowls full of grated cheese and diced avocado and lime quarters, and they ate sitting on the deckchairs as the tide came in further and the crowds slipped away. And as the fiery sun dropped to meet the horizon, Lily didn't give her phone a second thought, but sat and sipped her beer and gave a sigh of happiness.

This was real. This was family life. This was what perfection looked like. But nobody else needed to see it. Nobody else at all.

FAMILY FAVOURITE
RECIPES

*

*I*t's the end of the day. Everyone is tired but happy. New freckles have come out. Skin is sun-kissed and dried by the salt. There is sand between everyone's toes and in their hair. Bags full of soggy towels are dumped by the washing machine. Wetsuits are hung out to dry. Surfboards rinsed off and put away. It's time for a quick nap to recharge for the night ahead. Or a shower to rinse away the day's sun cream. Or to curl up with a book or a magazine.

This is my favourite time of day, when everyone is safely gathered in. I pull a cold bottle of Picpoul de Pinet from the fridge and pour a glass, light a scented candle, put on FIP FM – a cool French radio station that makes you feel as if you are in a film. I step into the garden to grab some herbs: outside the sea still shimmers and the sun is drifting away.

It's time to cook. Something easy but substantial that can be plonked on the table for us all to share. We'll chat about what we've done and what we're going to do. There'll be a few beers, maybe cocktails, certainly more wine.

And afterwards, maybe we'll wander back down to the beach for an ice cream and sit and watch the sun set for her well-deserved rest, for hopefully she has more work to do tomorrow.

Spicy lamb on flatbreads

This dish is hands-on and sociable: a piled-up platter of spicy lamb mince offset with a fresh salsa and herby yoghurt all scooped up with flatbreads.

SERVES 4

500g lamb mince (you could use beef if you can't get lamb)

1 tbsp olive oil

1 red onion, diced

2 garlic cloves, finely chopped

1 chilli, thinly sliced

3cm piece of fresh ginger, grated

2 tsp ground cumin

2 tsp ground coriander

1 tbsp tomato purée

1 × 400g tin chopped tomatoes

1 cucumber

2 tbsp pine kernels

Handful of chopped fresh mint and coriander

Juice of 1 lime

Flatbreads, to serve

For the herby yoghurt

250ml Greek yoghurt
2 garlic cloves, grated
Handful of chopped fresh mint

For the salsa

200g cherry tomatoes, halved
½ red onion, thinly sliced
1 tbsp pomegranate molasses
1 tsp balsamic vinegar

Dry-fry the mince in a pan until nicely browned and the fat has been released. Drain off the fat. In another pan, heat the olive oil and add the onion. When the onion starts to soften, add the garlic, chilli and ginger and cook for 5 minutes or so. Add the spices, cook for a minute then add the browned mince. When it's all starting to cook down, stir in the tomato purée and heat through, then add the tomatoes. Cook for 20 minutes, adding water if the mixture begins to dry out.

Make the herby yoghurt: put the yoghurt in a bowl and mix in the garlic and mint.

Trim the cucumber, cut in half down the middle, then slice each half lengthways and scoop out the seeds. Then cut the halves lengthways into long batons.

For the salsa, mix the cherry tomatoes and onion together and drizzle with the pomegranate molasses and vinegar, then leave to steep.

Dry-fry the pine kernels until they are nicely toasted.

Load up the spiced mince on a big plate. Scatter over the tomato salsa and pile up the cucumber batons. Drizzle over the herby yoghurt, then top with the pine kernels, mint and coriander, and squeeze over the lime juice.

Serve in bowls and scoop it all up with warmed flatbreads.

Dhal

This is for when you have been on the beach for just a little too long and are chilled to the bone. Its spicy warmness is the ultimate comfort food and it will restore your spirits even quicker than a hot bath. This version is quite mild, but you can add cayenne pepper, some chilli flakes or some garam masala if you like a bit of a kick.

We eat this dhal with naan bread or spooned into baked potatoes. Or you can make a lentil pie by topping the dhal with sweet potato mash. Dollops of Greek yoghurt are good with it too.

SERVES 4

1 tsp each coriander, mustard and cumin seeds

1 tbsp coconut oil

1 large red onion, chopped

3 garlic cloves, finely chopped

1 red chilli, finely diced

3cm piece fresh ginger, grated

1 tsp ground turmeric

Sea salt and freshly ground pepper

1 cinnamon stick

250g dried red lentils

1 × 400g tin chopped tomatoes

500ml vegetable or chicken stock

Juice of 1 lime

Handful of chopped fresh coriander

Dry-fry the seeds in a little pan for a couple of minutes to release their flavour, then crush them in a pestle and mortar.

Heat the coconut oil in a saucepan. Add the onion and fry until it starts to soften, then add the garlic, chilli and ginger. When starting to brown, add the crushed spices and turmeric and mix them together well until they form a fragrant paste. Add sea salt and freshly ground pepper to taste and the cinnamon stick. Tip in the lentils, coating them well in the paste, then pour on the tomatoes and stock. Once bubbling, turn down the heat and cook for 20 minutes or so, making sure the mixture doesn't burn or catch. If it's a little too thick add some more stock, or just water.

Just before serving, remove the cinnamon stick, squeeze over the lime juice and scatter with the coriander.

Courgette and halloumi fritters with herby dressing

I remember when Delia's Summer Collection came out and everyone went mad for her halloumi with lime and caper dressing – not many people had heard of the wonder cheese before then. I always keep a block or two in my fridge now, as it's so easy to throw it into a pan and then put in a salad or on a pile of roasted vegetables. These fritters are crispy, squeaky, salty perfection. I sometimes make mini versions to go with drinks. The herb dressing is a dream and can be used to liven up lots of things, so don't worry if you have some left over.

SERVES 4

2 medium courgettes

Sea salt

1 × 250g block halloumi

4 spring onions, thinly sliced

1 tbsp chopped fresh mint

1–2 tbsp panko breadcrumbs

1 egg, beaten

Sunflower oil, for frying

For the herb dressing

3 tbsps Greek yoghurt

3 tbsps mayonnaise

Juice and zest of one lime

1 small bunch chives

1 small bunch mint

1 small bunch flat leaf parsley

Grate the courgettes into a colander, sprinkle with sea salt and leave to drain for about 1 hour before squeezing out the excess liquid with your hands. Make sure they are really dry or your fritters will be soggy and limp.

Add the courgettes to a mixing bowl and grate in the halloumi. Add the spring onions, mint, breadcrumbs and egg, mixing well. If the mixture is still a little sticky, add some more breadcrumbs until it binds together. Shape into patties about 1cm thick then refrigerate for 30 minutes to firm them up. Heat the oil in a frying pan and fry the fritters for a couple of minutes each side until they are cooked through. Keep them warm in a low oven as you make them, wrapped in foil, until they are all done.

For the dressing, put all the ingrdients in a food processor or liquidiser and whizz until you have a lovely bright green sauce flecked with herbs.

Chicken souvlaki wraps with tzatziki

We were mad on fajitas for a long time – a Friday night favourite – but one day I hit upon this slight twist to ring the changes. We used to have our souvlaki in pitta bread but wraps work just as well and somehow it's easier to get more extras in! Do the marinade in the morning if you can remember so the flavours get a chance to develop.

SERVES 4

4 large chicken breasts, cut into chunks

2 tbsp olive oil

I tsp sea salt

2 garlic cloves, finely chopped

Zest and juice of I lemon

I tbsp dried oregano

I tbsp dried mint

I tsp ground turmeric

4 tortilla wraps

200g cherry tomatoes, halved

I red onion, thinly sliced

I tbsp pitted black olives, halved

Handful of chopped fresh mint

For the tzatziki

1 cucumber
250 ml Greek yoghurt
1 garlic clove, grated
1 tbsp chopped fresh mint
Zest and juice of 1 lemon
Sea salt and freshly ground black pepper

Combine the chicken, oil, salt, garlic, lemon zest and juice, herbs and turmeric in a large bowl. Leave to marinate for at least 1 hour.

Make the tzatziki: slice the cucumber down the middle, scoop out the seeds and dice into small pieces. Add the cucumber pieces to the Greek yoghurt, along with the garlic, mint and lemon zest and juice, and stir thoroughly.

Heat a heavy-bottomed non-stick frying pan and tip in the chicken together with the marinade. Fry until thoroughly cooked through but still tender, 10–15 minutes – cut into a thick piece to make sure there is no pink – and the marinade has reduced a little. Don't overcook the chicken – you want it nice and moist, not dry.

Warm the wraps in the oven. Scatter with the tomatoes, onion and olives, then the chicken and top with tzatziki. Garnish with the mint, roll up the wraps and enjoy!

Lime pie with sea salt

As I said, we don't often bother with pudding, but if there are hungry guests then this creamy lime pie is super-easy and always a winner, though it does need a couple of hours to chill to be at its best so make it ahead.

SERVES 8

150g digestive biscuits or ginger nuts

150g butter, melted, plus extra for greasing

100g white chocolate

Zest and juice of 5 limes

1 × 397g tin condensed milk

300ml double cream

1 × 250g can squirty cream

Sea salt

Preheat the oven to 150°C/fan 130°C/gas mark 2 and grease and line with parchment paper a 20cm springform cake tin. (This cheesecake can be difficult to lift out so I sometimes just serve it on the bottom of the tin once the outside has been removed.)

Smash up the biscuits into fine sand and mix thoroughly with the butter before pressing firmly into the prepared tin. Bake in the oven for 10 minutes. Cool thoroughly.

Melt the white chocolate in a bowl over a saucepan of boiling water. Pour the chocolate over the cooled digestive base until completely covered. Put in the fridge to harden off.

Keep back one lime's worth of zest for decoration. In a large bowl, stir the rest of the lime zest and juice into the condensed milk. Whip the double cream until it is just holding its shape and fold it carefully into the condensed milk mixture, then pour into the tin. Chill for 4 hours until firm.

When you are ready to serve, remove the outer ring of the tin and cover the pie with squirty cream. Sprinkle on the reserved lime zest and scatter with sea salt.

THE TEN BEST
BEACH HUT BOARD GAMES

Everyone's fed but not yet ready to go to bed, so it's time to crack open another bottle of wine, light the wood burner and dig out the board games, bringing out people's competitive spirit and revealing their true characters. Are they strategic? Sneaky? Bad losers? Do they have an astonishing amount of general knowledge or a massive vocabulary that you had no idea of? Or are they great team players? Get to know the truth about your friends and family in a short space of time …

CLUEDO

The classic detective game which engages your little grey cells as you find out who murdered Dr Black – Miss Scarlet in the library with a wrench?

TICKET TO RIDE

Collect the appropriate cards for train tracks, tunnels, ferries and stations to make your way from city to city across eighteenth-century Europe.

MONOPOLY

The ultimate in empire building; settle yourself in for the long haul and Do Not Pass Go.

TRIVIAL PURSUIT

Brush up on your general knowledge for this competitive classic as you collect pieces of the iconic pie.

YOU'VE GOT CRABS

Use secret signals to gain points – subterfuge, deception and hilarity ensue.

SCRABBLE

Wordsmiths unite – but it's not always the one with the biggest vocabulary who wins if you can hit that triple word score.

CARDS AGAINST HUMANITY

Somewhat X-rated, ask a question from a black card and opponents choose the most (least) appropriate answer from their white card. Ruuuuude. For older members of the family only.

EXPLODING KITTENS
Highly strategic feline Russian roulette game of defusing kittens – but if they explode, you're out!

PASS THE PIGS
Throw the little piggies and win or lose points depending on how the pigs land. This is such a simple game but so endearing. And very portable – you can carry it in your pocket.

ARTICULATE
Bring everyone out of their shell with this fast-talking game of description – the few rules are fiendishly hard to obey.

At the end of the day, you can't beat a good old-fashioned jigsaw. It's surprising how the least likely person can become obsessed with completing a metre-square 1000 piece picture of baked beans. Silence reigns as everyone bows their head over the puzzle in search of the perfect fit. It's the ideal way to pass the time as the rain drums on the roof of your beach hut. Cocoa and shortbread compulsory.

A romantic
dinner for two

As the Sun Goes Down

Lewis left Sofia curled up on the couch having a late afternoon nap while he unpacked all the goodies from the cooler.

Behind her, the balloons he'd ordered to be waiting in the hut drifted lazily in the breeze from the open door. They formed an arch of pale metallic pink, rose gold, silver and grey. He'd worried that it was a bit over the top, but actually they looked very pretty against the white wooden walls. In the middle was a dark pink heart: he thought of it as his heart, the heart he had given to her the first time he'd seen her ordering a drink at the bar in the Red Lion. He thought she looked like an angel, with her peroxide white ringlets dip-dyed pink at the bottom, and he couldn't take his eyes off her. And then he saw her grab the walking stick that had been leaning up against the bar, and make her way back to her mates, and that was it. He was smitten.

It was weird, because it was usually girls who chased

him. He wasn't classically handsome – he was never going to be lean, and he'd shaved all his hair off the moment he'd caught a glimpse of scalp, and he was very freckly – but he had a Robbie Williams cheekiness that was very alluring. He never kept his girlfriends for long, though. He hated being tied down. Hated it when they started trying to move things around in his flat, or dictate where they went on holiday. His mates were all settling down, and he didn't envy them one bit. He loved his freedom.

But the moment he saw Sofia, he felt something he'd never felt before. She'd turned and looked at him. She looked startled, as if she felt it too. Then she'd scowled.

She was about to sit down but instead she walked over to him. He could see she was unsteady, though not in pain. It wasn't an injury. It was something she'd learned to live with. She stood in front of him. She had a heart-shaped face and bewitching hazel eyes with ridiculously long eyelashes. He knew enough about women to know they weren't real, but they didn't look trashy. She was wearing a Guns N' Roses sweatshirt, ripped jeans and emerald-green cowboy boots. An angelic tomboy. He liked her style, although he couldn't define it. Definitely unconventional. An arty edge.

'What?' she said. 'You're staring at me. What is it?'

She was half belligerent, half teasing. And a little bit drunk. He couldn't speak. He was never at a loss for words when it came to women. But she made him tongue-tied. He could feel her spirit and her attitude. It was bouncing off him, like being brushed by nettles or touching an electric fence.

'I feel like I know you,' he managed at last.

'Well, you don't,' she scoffed, and swept her gaze up and down him, taking in his rough collarless linen shirt, his jeans and waxed boots. He too had a definite style – urban country, he called it. You had to be image-conscious in his line of business.

'No. I know I don't. But I *feel* like I do. Does that make sense?' What an awful chat-up line. What a pillock.

She raised an eyebrow. She had great eyebrows. Strong. 'Not really.'

'What's your name?'

'Sofia.' She didn't ask his. She wasn't interested. But why had she come over, in that case? There was definitely something. She was playing hard to get. He could play that game too.

'Sorry. I didn't mean to hassle you.' He turned to walk away.

'Hey.' He felt a prod on the back of his leg. She'd poked him with her walking stick. He turned back. She looked annoyed. 'Don't walk away from me. Tell me your name.'

'Lewis.' Her eyebrow went up again. 'My mum's a big *Inspector Morse* fan.'

That made her laugh. 'What do you do?'

'What is this?' He raised *his* eyebrows. 'An interview? Try and guess.'

She put her head on one side, surveying him, her eyes sparkling. 'I'd say ... you own a barber shop. One of those trendy ones. All bare brick and beaten-up leather chairs.'

How did she know? She must have inside information. She was bang-on. Except he actually had two, and was about to open a third, a concession in the city's biggest department store. Someone in the pub must have told her. He was a fixture in here. He grinned.

'Who told you that, then?'

'I work at Moodys. They're very excited. I saw you at the planning meeting.'

He shook his head. 'I'd have remembered you.'

'I was in my work kit. Leggings and a hoodie. My hair was in a beanie.'

'So what do you do?'

'I'm their visual merchandiser. I'll be doing your fit.'

He felt prickly. He was very possessive about what he had created. He was proud to have one of his salons in Moodys – they were very fussy about who they took on. He wasn't sure if she was winding him up.

'I get final approval, don't forget. I had that written into the contract. I've got to protect my brand.'

She touched him on the arm. The warmth shot through him.

'Don't worry,' she said. 'You're in safe hands. I totally respect what you're doing. I think it's great.'

They locked eyes. He swallowed. This was weird. Girls never made him feel like this. She leaned in.

'I did feel something, when I saw you,' she told him. Her voice was low and husky and he imagined it whispering secrets. 'I never usually feel anything. I've trained myself not to.'

This felt like a confession. He frowned. Her words made him feel uncomfortable. 'Why?'

'I've got MS,' she told him. 'It's not anyone's idea of fun. Sometimes I can't walk. Sometimes I can't even talk. Sometimes I can't stay awake. I might end up in a wheelchair. So I don't really do *relationships*.'

She put a bitter emphasis on the last word. Her eyes darkened; hardened. He knew his reaction would be key to what happened next. Whether he'd have this girl in his life or not.

He shrugged. 'Why not? It's not catching, is it?'

She flinched. For a moment, he thought he'd been too flippant. He always used humour when he didn't really know what to say. But then she laughed. So hard she nearly bent double. And he joined in. They were laughing together and it was a wonderful, conspiratorial, gleeful laugh of the kind that bonds you immediately.

'So, will you have a drink with me?' he asked.

'Yes,' she said, nodding, still laughing, looking at him in disbelief.

And here they were, two years later. She was the

most difficult, fragile, tough, funny, creative, impossible woman he'd ever met. And the sexiest. He still felt a rush of desire when he looked at her. He was looking at her now, stretched out, her hair tumbling everywhere, those ridiculous eyelashes resting on her cheeks.

They were so good together. They spent most of their time taking the mickey out of each other. They had the same irreverent sense of humour. But underneath the mickey-taking was a deep passion. They both understood each other's drive for success and independence. They both pushed the boundaries of their creativity. She loved her job as a visual merchandiser – 'just a posh term for a window dresser, really' – and she wanted to live and work in Paris. 'But I don't speak French, so I'm learning. *L'autobus part à midi. Où est la piscine?*'

And he learned, very quickly, how to deal with her illness, and the toll it took on her. He could measure it better than she could now. He could read her physically. He could see the strain in her face; the energy drain from her. He was always there to catch her.

Today was her birthday. Her thirtieth birthday. And she didn't want a party. The relapses were too unpredictable lately. They were getting more frequent, which meant she might not have the energy to go if they did organise one. Worse, she might have one of the bouts of depression that enveloped her, left her pinned under the duvet unable to get up. So he'd planned a week by the sea as a surprise. If she wasn't up to it, when the time came, he would just cancel. But when her birthday came around, she was in a good place, physically and mentally. He told her what to pack, and they set off, and she had no idea where they were going.

He would never forget the look on her face when she saw the row of huts lining the beach.

'You're kidding. We've got one of these? Oh my God!' She had tumbled out of the car, suddenly full of an energy she'd managed to summon from somewhere. 'You bloody legend. This is a dream come true. I've always wanted to stay in a beach hut.'

Her joy made his heart burst. She was like a child, overwhelmed with excitement. She couldn't wait to get in the sea. In the water, her body seemed to do whatever she wanted it to.

'It's like being cradled,' she said. 'The water just holds me. It's just so relaxing. I can't tell you.'

She lay, staring up at the sky, and he felt so proud to have found her some respite from her pain. She was like a different person. Her face looked even more beautiful, if that was possible. The water had washed the strain away.

And then it was evening. Time for him to prepare her birthday dinner. He was no cook, so he'd called on one of his mates who was a chef for advice.

'Bear in mind I can't really cook, remember. I mean, I

can do the basics, but nothing fancy. And the beach hut's only got a little stove.'

'What are her favourite things?' Gary asked, and Lewis had told him. Goat's cheese. Raspberries. White chocolate. And she was a pescatarian.

He'd thought Gary had forgotten, and he didn't want to pester him because he knew he worked unsociable hours and probably didn't want to think about food when he got off. But just before they left, Gary had turned up with a cool box full to the brim with all the ingredients he needed for Sofia's birthday dinner, together with instructions.

Lewis was overwhelmed. Life could be cruel. Incredibly cruel. But people could be kind.

'Bloody hell, mate. Thanks. I don't know how to repay you.'

'Just give her a good time.' Gary nodded at him. Everyone loved Sofia. They knew how tough life was for her. They knew she could be a total bitch, and that when she felt bad she pushed people away. But they were always there for her when she came back around.

Lewis put the table outside on the sand and covered it with a white tablecloth that reached the ground. He'd found a candelabra in a charity shop. It looked suitably theatrical and over the top. He set two places, and put two Lloyd Loom chairs from the hut on either side, piling them up with cushions. Then an ice bucket, for the champagne that would accompany ...

He panicked and patted his pocket to make sure the packet was still there, then smiled in relief. Everything was perfect. Behind him, the sea was gently nudging its way up to high tide. Most of the day-trippers had gone, leaving just the hardcore further along the beach. The table reminded him of the opening scene of *Jurassic Park*. One of their favourite movies. They watched a lot of films: his flat was done out like a home cinema, with a huge screen and plush seating and a cocktail bar, a bachelor luxury that had actually turned out to be perfect for snuggling up when Sofia felt less than her best.

He headed back inside to prepare the food, yet again grateful for Gary's generosity. Everything was packaged up in courses, neatly labelled and with written instructions so he couldn't go wrong. Gary had even written out the menu: roasted figs with goat's cheese, drizzled with honey. Salmon on a bed of samphire (he wasn't sure quite what that was but Gary had provided it). A white chocolate cake with raspberries. A sexy, romantic dinner for two, perfect for …

She was waking. 'Hey, sleepyhead,' he said. 'Why don't you go and take a shower? Get dressed for dinner. It's going to be something special.'

'With you cooking?' She looked doubtful, but he wasn't hurt. His lack of skill in the kitchen was no secret.

He pointed at her. 'You're going to be blown away. Go on. Go and get ready. Dinner will be served at eight.'

For the next hour, he wrestled with the tiny kitchen and got everything prepped and ready. And bang on eight o'clock she appeared. She was wearing a pale-green chiffon halterneck dress that fell to the floor, her hair loose over her shoulders. He couldn't speak. She smiled at him as she walked to the doorway, and he held his breath as she made it without stumbling or faltering. He walked over and took her arm nevertheless.

'Let me escort you to your table, madam.'

He led her down the steps and watched her face as she saw what he had done outside. Her eyes shone like the sparkling sea in the evening sun. '*Jurassic Park*,' she laughed. 'It's just like the opening of *Jurassic Park*.'

'Damn, you're good,' he said, pulling out her chair for her to sit down. 'Let me get your cocktail.'

He came back with a tray bearing two Strawberry Mules. 'Happy birthday,' he said to her, and she laughed, obviously delighted although she pretended not to like slushy, romantic gestures.

Dinner was perfect. He managed to roast the figs so the cheese was golden and bubbling, and the salmon was tender, the samphire crunchy – he'd followed Gary's instructions to the letter – and he couldn't mess up the cake, because it was all done for him.

'How did you pull this off?' Sofia asked. 'You can't cook to save your life.'

He tapped his nose as he opened a bottle of champagne.

His stomach was churning. He couldn't back out of what he was planning to do next. When would he ever get a chance like this again? A perfect day; a romantic meal; the sun setting over the sea? He felt in his pocket. He'd spent days wandering in and out of every antiques and jewellery shop in town, before settling on an opal cocktail ring. It was iridescent, a pale milky green, like the full moon, shimmering with flecks of hidden gold. Mysterious. Not flashy, because Sofia wasn't a flashy type. She valued style over carats. But it was a statement. He was sure she'd like it.

'Sofia,' he said as he handed her a glass of champagne, and she frowned, because he looked serious, and he was never serious. 'I've lured you here under false pretences. This isn't just a birthday dinner. This is ... me wanting to ask you a question. You are the most amazing person I've ever met. Every day you surprise me. Every day I fall in love with you a little bit more. Every day your strength and bravery and your *balls* make me wish I was a better man. But I hope I'm good enough. Good enough to be ...' She narrowed her eyes as he fumbled for the words. 'Good enough to be your husband.' He snapped open the ring box he'd pulled out of his pocket and the opal gleamed in the last light of the sun. He took it out with shaking hands. 'Will you marry me?'

Time stood still as she stared at him. The colour had drained from her face. Her eyes were hard. There was no delight. No joy. She smashed both her hands down on the table and Lewis jumped.

'No,' she shouted. 'I don't want to bloody marry you. I don't want to look at your face when you realise what a mistake you've made. I don't want to drag you down. I don't want you having to ... push my bloody wheelchair.'

'Sofia!' Lewis was shocked by the force of her reaction. He could see she was trying to stand up, but she couldn't. They'd done too much. The journey. The swimming. They should have had an early night.

Shit. She'd fallen over. She was lying in a heap and he could feel her despair. He rushed over to pick her up and she threw a handful of sand at him.

'You've bloody ruined it,' she said, and she crumpled, exhausted, sobbing.

'You're going to bed,' he said, bending down and wrapping his arms around her. There was no point in arguing now. She was rigid with tension and rage. She was too weak to fight him, although he could feel her wanting to. He held her until she finally gave in and relaxed.

He carried her inside, thinking how much he loved this bundle of attitude and energy; the very smell of her, salt and vanilla. He loved her strength and her vulnerability. Her fury and her softness. He didn't want a normal relationship that went in a straight line. He lived for the challenge of the ups and downs. He'd learned to read her and her disease. He'd learned how, between the three of them, they could give her the best life possible. It was always a challenge. It was never boring. It was intense and passionate and … the most meaningful thing that had ever happened to him.

'I can't do this any more,' she said as he took her to the tiny bedroom at the back of the hut. 'I can't pretend this is a normal relationship. I'm done. We're done. I'm going home tomorrow. You can find someone else to marry. There'll be hundreds of them to choose from. You could have whoever you want. You deserve a normal life.'

He didn't say anything. He didn't argue with her. He laid her down on the bed, helped her take off her dress, pulled her nightshirt over her head, pulled back the duvet and tucked her under. He sat on the bed until she fell asleep, waiting for her breathing to even and her pulse to lower. Then he went and cleared everything away, washed up, dried up and wrapped up the remains of the cake.

When order was restored, he poured the last of the champagne into a glass and sat outside looking up at the sky, balefully black until eventually it relented and gave him the gift of a thousand stars. Around him, music and laughter drifted out from the other beach huts. The waves whispered to him and he listened hard to what they had to say, for they had centuries of wisdom, the certainty of the tide. They spoke the truth. And when he'd drained the last drop of golden bubbles, he went back into the hut and undressed, sliding into bed next to her.

He reached out for her right hand in the dark, explored the back of it gently until he found the finger he wanted, then slid the ring onto it. It was hers, whether she wanted to marry him or not. It wasn't a conditional gift. He certainly wasn't going to take it back. It was beautiful, like she was, and it belonged to her. He curled himself around her and drifted off to sleep.

In the morning he woke up and found her awake, staring at the ceiling. He looked down at her right hand. The ring was gone. He opened his mouth to say something, to explain that he didn't expect anything, but she reached out and put a finger on his lips.

'Shhh,' she said, and lifted her left hand. There it was. On her engagement finger. 'I'm sorry I was such a wally last night. Sometimes it just gets too much and I can't handle it. I can't think straight. Of course I'll marry you. Of course I will.'

RECIPES FOR A
ROMANTIC DINNER
FOR TWO

*I*t's the archetypal romantic setting – a table for two on the sand, with a white cloth and a candelabra, the waves gently lapping just beside you, and the sun in the distance dropping into the sea. Of course, for it to be perfect there would be a white-gloved butler to hand, twisting the cork and bringing out oysters on a silver tray, then discreetly melting into the background while you stare into each other's eyes sipping champagne. But in the absence of staff, this menu is perfect for an al fresco supper *à deux* – with a little preparation beforehand it doesn't take much work, especially if you don't have elaborate cooking facilities, and the colours look very pretty on a white plate. Leaving plenty of time to make sure the ring box is secreted in the perfect place for it to be produced with a flourish!

Strawberry mule

This luscious pink cocktail is the perfect start to your evening, saved from too much sweetness by the lime. And strawberries mean summer, don't they?

SERVES 2

7 large ripe strawberries
Juice of 1 lime
1 tsp sugar
2 mint leaves, plus 2 sprigs to decorate
100ml vodka
Ginger beer, chilled

Muddle 6 of the strawberries, the lime juice, sugar and mint in the bottom of a glass until broken down and the flavours released. Add the vodka and strain into a fresh pair of glasses. Top up with ginger beer. Halve the remaining strawberry and use to decorate the glasses along with a sprig of mint.

Roasted figs

Plump, luscious and fragant, figs are the perfect prelude
to a romantic encounter. The nuts and cheese balance the
sweetness of the figs and honey. This starter is super easy
so it won't keep you from the table for too long.

SERVES 2

4 ripe but firm figs

80g fresh goat's cheese, crumbled

1 tbsp runny honey

4 pecan nuts, chopped

Preheat the oven to 200°C/fan 180°C/gas mark 6 and line
a baking sheet with parchment paper.

Wash the figs and cut off the tips then cut a cross in the
top of each, pressing so it opens like a bird's beak. Push the
goat's cheese into the opening and transfer to the baking
sheet. Drizzle the honey over the figs, then sprinkle over the
chopped nuts. Roast in the oven for about 5 minutes until
everything starts to melt and mingle.

Salmon with samphire

The prettiest supper – pink and green – and also very easy.
There should be some left over, in which case it is gorgeous
cold the next day served with any remaining potatoes
crushed with the sauce drizzled over.

SERVES 2

1 × 450g half salmon side

1 tbsp butter

2 lemons

Several dill sprigs

200g Jersey Royals, scrubbed

200g samphire

For the dressing

3 tbsp sour cream

3 tbsp mayonnaise

Zest and juice of 1 lemon

1 tbsp each chopped fresh parsley, chives and tarragon

Sea salt and freshly ground black pepper

Preheat the oven to 200°C/fan 180°C/gas mark 6.

First, make the dressing: whizz the sour cream, mayonnaise, lemon zest and juice, herbs and seasoning in a food processor.

Place the salmon in a large piece of foil in a baking dish. Dot with the butter and sprinkle over some sea salt. Slice 1½ of the lemons thickly and cover the salmon with the slices. Scatter over the dill. Wrap the foil loosely over the salmon and bake in the oven for 15 minutes. Check it is cooked through to pale pink before removing. Keep warm under the foil.

Boil the potatoes in salted water for 10–15 minutes until tender.

Boil the samphire for 2–3 minutes.

Serve slices of the salmon on a bed of samphire with the potatoes on the side. Drizzle the salmon with the dressing and squeeze over the remaining ½ lemon.

White chocolate and raspberry cake

This cake comes a very, very close second to the orange and almond cake as being my favourite. It doesn't look like much but it's rather good-natured, like the best sort of friend! It's gooey with a crispy edge, and you can throw whatever fruit you like into it and it doesn't mind. I love raspberries but blueberries are good too, or a mixture of both if you feel so inclined. It keeps well too.

MAKES 1 CAKE

250g butter
200g white chocolate
300g golden caster sugar
1 tsp vanilla essence
300ml full-fat milk
250g self-raising flour, sifted
½ tsp bicarbonate of soda
2 large eggs, beaten
400g fresh raspberries
Crème fraîche, to serve

Preheat the oven to 160°C/fan 140°C/gas mark 3 and grease and line a 23cm cake tin.

Melt the butter in a saucepan then add the white chocolate and sugar, stirring until everything is melted, then take off the heat. Mix the vanilla essence with the milk and add to the chocolate mixture gradually, stirring to cool it down. Fold in the flour and bicarbonate of soda, then stir through the eggs. You will have a very wet batter but don't worry! Drop in half the raspberries and mix in very gently so as not to break them. Pour into the tin and bake for 1 hour. Check that a knife inserted in the centre comes out clean before removing from the oven. Leave for 30 minutes in the tin before tipping out onto a wire rack to cool completely.

Serve with the rest of the raspberries and dollops of crème fraîche.

THE TOP TEN
BEACH MOVIES

You've eaten your fill, drunk the last drop of wine and watched the sun set. Now it's time to snuggle up on the sofa together under a cosy blanket and watch a movie, preferably one set by the sea.

FOR ALL THE FAMILY

Finding Nemo
Clownfish Marlin searches for his kidnapped son, Nemo, with the help of his aquatic companions.

The Little Mermaid
Mermaid Ariel dreams of becoming human and falls in love with Prince Eric – leading her to make a deal with an evil sea witch.

ICONIC SURFING MOVIES

Blue Crush

After an accident, chambermaid/surfer girl Anne Marie decides to get back in the game with the help of her friends.

Point Break

Johnny Utah is an FBI agent investigating a gang of surfers he believes to be bank robbers.

ROMANTIC COMEDY

Something's Gotta Give

Diane Keaton and Jack Nicholson as total opposites who fall for each other in later life in an idyllic Hamptons setting.

Mamma Mia

A woman meets the three possible fathers of her daughter on a Greek island with plenty of music from Abba!

Splash

A young man falls in love with a mermaid, with ensuing complications.

ACTION ADVENTURE

Cast Away

Chuck Noland is washed up on a deserted Pacific island and has to quickly learn how to survive.

The Beach

Adventure-seeking Richard is given a map in Thailand to find the ultimate paradise – but it turns out to be not quite heaven when he gets there.

From Here to Eternity

The trials and tribulations of three US Army soldiers and the women in their lives in the run-up to the attack on Pearl Harbor.

Nightcap

A Difficult Choice

Everdene was Jenna's favourite pitch. On a day like this, it was a goldmine. There'd be a steady stream of customers, eager for the cool of an ice cream on a hot day. There was every chance she would run out by lunchtime. She'd have to drive back home to stock up her freezers again for the evening trade.

She still couldn't believe the success of her little business. Her van was a familiar fixture on the sea front, and she was well-known. The Ice-cream Girl, they called her, and sometimes she sang for them, dressed up in her vintage frocks, belting out Dusty Springfield or Amy Winehouse.

Though she wouldn't be able to fit into her frocks for much longer. She thought she'd just manage until the end of the summer, but any minute now she would have to pack them all away. She was half excited, half terrified by the prospect of motherhood, unsure how it was going to fit in. The baby was due in September, so she would have a good few months to get used to being a mum before she got back behind the wheel of the van after Easter. Would she manage to juggle it all?

Craig, her husband, had reassured her. If it didn't work, they could sell the van and the goodwill for a decent sum. But Jenna didn't want to give it up. It was living proof that she had made something of herself, after a rocky start. It was her identity. She thought it was going to be okay. Her mum had promised to look after the baby. There was a time when Jenna wouldn't have relied on her mother for anything, but they were close these days. Everything had worked out. People could change. They both had.

It could so easily have gone the other way. She cringed as she remembered how low she had sunk; how desperate she had become at her situation. It was on this very beach, and if Craig hadn't caught her, how long might she have gone on, nicking stuff out of people's bags when they were in the water? She'd been unaware that the handsome policeman had been watching her from his beach hut, until she'd felt his hand on her shoulder.

And now, they were married. Both of their lives had changed that day. He'd seen something in her, something more than what she had believed herself to be: a loser, a chancer. It turned out she was a fighter.

Today was her last day serving ice cream. Craig had insisted she should have some time off before the baby was born. A few golden weeks of sunshine, relaxing, pottering, nesting. She had protested, thinking she would get bored, that she would only worry, but actually, now the day had come, she was grateful. It was getting harder to move around and, by the end of the day, she was exhausted. She had her two loyal assistants taking over from her, and she could supervise them from afar. She was grateful for the chance of some downtime.

She looked at her queue of customers, and felt pride and a surge of emotion. She swallowed down the lump in her throat, smiled and slid back the window.

'Let's be having you, then,' she called out, her scoop at the ready. 'What can I get you?'

∞

Elspeth stepped up to the window, hoping she'd remembered what they all wanted. She felt a little bit guilty that they were working so hard on what should be their holiday, but they had risen to the occasion with enthusiasm. She hardly recognised the hut already! Meg was obsessed with television makeover shows, and had written out a time-plan and a checklist.

'By the end of the week, this hut will be transformed,' she told her grandmother. It was long overdue, she knew. She was impressed with Meg's skills. She was even more handy than the boys, juggling hammer and nails and screwdrivers with dexterity and bossing them around.

Two big tins of paint were waiting for the exterior makeover. The four of them had stood in the DIY shop, arguing over what colour to paint it. Stripes won through in the end. A fresh minty green and white, to cover over the boring brown.

And during the upheaval, Meg had found the photographs in the back of the cupboard. There they were, memories of a golden day, stuck in an old envelope. Elspeth had leafed through them, Meg exclaiming at the antics and the outfits. Louche blond Dickon and his twin Octavia, lolling on the sand. Black-haired Juliet, smoking as always, hidden behind her sunglasses. And Elspeth herself, looking slightly out of place in her blue cotton frock.

'These are so cool! Oh my God, look at this!' Meg held up the photo of the human pyramid. 'We should put them onto canvas. They would look amazing on the wall.'

'Why not?' smiled Elspeth. She could still remember standing on Octavia and Juliet, desperately trying to keep her balance, arms out. She could still remember falling. What if she hadn't fallen? What if she'd gone back to Oxford with Dickon that evening? What if Harry had ended up marrying Octavia? A whole different set of children would be in the hut now, instead of her wonderful three.

'One Nobbly Bobbly, one Twister and two 99s,' she asked Jenna. How many ice creams had she bought from her over the past years? 'How are you doing?'

Jenna puffed out her cheeks. 'It's my last day today.

I'm going on maternity leave.' She rolled her eyes slightly, as if it was something to be ashamed of.

'Enjoy the chance to relax.' Elspeth smiled. 'You're going to be a lovely mum.'

'Thanks. I hope so,' said Jenna, handing over the change, then she smiled at the next customer.

∞

'Can I have a Magnum, please? White chocolate.'

'Coming up.'

Sofia reached out her hand with the money, admiring the sight of the opal on her finger. It felt good to see it there. She hadn't noticed it at first when she woke. The sea air had made her sleep more soundly than she had done for months, and she'd opened her eyes just after nine. For a moment she lay enjoying the sound of the waves, and the cry of the seagulls, and then she went to brush her hair away from her eyes and caught sight of the ring on her right hand.

She had lain there for some time, staring at it. Feeling him breathing next to her.

The truth was, Lewis had taken her unawares the night before, and she'd panicked. Sofia always liked being in control. It was a fault, she knew. But it was only because she was so very much *not* in control of her body. It was a survival tactic.

Now, in the soft light of the early morning, she knew

what was the right thing to do. She felt overwhelmed. She had never thought she would find someone who would want to share her life. But Lewis never made her feel anything less than perfect, even when she kicked off like she had last night. Did she deserve him? Did he, more to the point, deserve her?

But as she looked at him sleeping, she knew the answer. She had to believe. After all, he made her a better person. He'd taught her patience, and how to look after herself, and how to stop before she got too tired. She slid the ring off her right hand and transferred it over to her left. And when he woke, she told him she would marry him.

And then the day carried on as normal. Lewis went for a surfing lesson, and Sofia sat outside the hut listening to music with her earphones in, dozing in the sun, until she got too hot and decided to go for an ice cream. It wasn't too far to the van. She was taking it easy today. Yesterday had probably been too much. The journey, the swimming, dinner ... the proposal.

She looked in admiration at the girl serving the ice creams. She was dressed in a fifties halterneck, red with white polka dots, and was obviously expecting a baby. She was luminous – she looked so happy, talking to all the customers, joking and laughing. Comfortable in her skin.

Sofia caught her breath. She had to admit it to herself. It was what she wanted. For a long time, she had pretended she wasn't interested in becoming a mother. It seemed easiest that way. But suddenly, she thought it might be a possibility. It would be hard, but not impossible. And she knew that Lewis would make it happen for her. She knew he would move mountains if she wanted a family. She knew he would always be there.

There was a lump in her throat. The first step was admitting to herself that was what she wanted.

'Hey.' The girl was looking at her, holding out her Magnum. 'Are you okay?'

'Oh! Yes. Thank you.' Sofia reached out and took it. 'Sorry. Away with the fairies.'

The second step would be to voice her desire to Lewis. She'd talk to him when he got back from his surfing lesson. She had the feeling he would want a baby just as much as she did.

◌

It was easier than she thought. Not that she had a choice, for her phone was completely ruined from its dip in the rock pool. Short of making Reg drive her to the retail park to buy a replacement, Lily couldn't take a photograph if she wanted to.

But it was strange, retraining her brain. For a start, this would be brilliant for her Instagram Stories – pictures of all the different ice creams they were ordering. And the girl in the van looked amazing. Lily would definitely have asked if she could take her photo: she was Instagram-ready in her polka-dot dress and her mini-beehive and perfectly flicked eyeliner.

But she didn't. Instead, Lily helped Elsie and Zak peruse the poster on the front of the van and choose what they wanted. Old her would have left them to it while she pecked out hashtags. This time, she debated the merits of a Twister versus a Solero with Elsie.

'I reckon a Solero would last longer,' she told her daughter. 'But you have what you want. And we're here all week, don't forget. You can have something different every day.'

She looked at the beach. The golden sand, the shimmering sea, the wonky line of brightly coloured huts. Why would she want to be in Ibiza? She shuddered at the memory of the evening at the airport hotel, how out of place and awkward she had felt. Okay, so she wasn't drifting about in a gauzy kaftan and high heels, sipping on a cocktail, looking forward to dinner at a swanky restaurant followed by a night of dancing. But she had treasured every moment of last night. They'd stayed up until late playing board games, then she and Reg had sat out on the steps with a bottle of wine once the kids had fallen into bed, and they'd talked out what she could do.

She was going to go back to college. She was going to do a foundation course in art and see where it took her. And she was going to help out with the plumbing business on the side. Reg had wanted to take someone else on for a while so he could get through his backlog more quickly, and if he had Lily's support it would be much easier. Someone to send out quotes and invoices and keep his Facebook page updated. And do a proper job of marketing. Organise a new wrap for the van. Get him some business cards. All the stuff she was good at. Without falling down the rabbit hole again …

She was pretty sure she could do that. She had got things into perspective now. She could learn how to use social media without it taking over their lives. She already felt a million times more relaxed. She realised that she had been going through life without enjoying a single moment of it, contrary to what she was displaying on her feed. It had been hell, the drive and the panic, the constant comparisons with other people, trying to get ahead of the game.

'Mum, can we get some bodyboards?' Zak looked up at her, his little face eager. They'd seen other kids in the water, zooming along, catching the waves.

Normally, she'd try to figure out how to get them for free. She'd be setting up a photoshoot at the water's edge, with the brand name in full view. And before they knew it, the day would be gone and there'd be no time left for fun. But now, they had all the time in the world.

'Why not?' she said. 'I'm going to get one too.'

When had she last done that? Spent the day playing with her kids, without checking her phone every two minutes? She couldn't remember. She felt ashamed. But it wasn't too late.

They took their ice creams and wandered up the path to the shops, looking at the kites and buckets and spades and hula hoops. She thought fleetingly of the hotel in Ibiza, with its infinity pool and canopied day beds and twenty-four-hour cocktail service, and realised how very lucky she was to have escaped.

☙

'A salted caramel cone,' said Anna. 'With nuts. How's it going, Jenna? How long have you got?'

'This is my last day,' said Jenna, digging her scoop into the tub of ice cream. 'I'm going to be a normal holidaymaker for the rest of the summer.'

'Well, if you want to hang out, this is my day off. Every week.' Anna grinned. She had the latest Maggie O'Farrell novel in her bag and was going to sit and read for the rest of the day.

'I'd love that,' said Jenna. The two of them had often compared notes, being in a similar business. They went out to the Ship Aground sometimes, if there was a band on. Jenna handed Anna her cone. 'Listen, Dino's back. I saw him last night.'

'Yeah,' said Anna. 'He came sniffing around yesterday afternoon. I think he expected me to drop everything and come crawling back.'

'You're not going to, right?' Jenna looked worried. She'd seen what Dino had done to Anna when he left.

'No way.' Anna took a lick of her ice cream. Sweet, sticky, salty, creamy perfection. 'He won't be staying round here long. Everyone knows his game now. You know how fast word travels in Everdene.'

'I sure do.' Jenna nodded, and looked around at all the holidaymakers. That was the beauty of it. Everyone here looked out for each other. If you needed something, you only had to say. There was a tight network among the local business owners. Everything could be sorted. She leaned forward to Anna, eyes sparkling. 'Listen, we're doing a bit of a barbie tonight at the beach hut. Craig's got one of his mates coming down from up country. He's pretty smoking hot.' She did a chef's kiss.

'I'd love that.' Anna smiled her acceptance.

That was just what she needed. A few beers, a barbecue, a bit of flirtation. The promise of life after Dino was as sweet as the ice cream starting to melt in her hand.

∞

Later that afternoon, Jenna scraped the last spoonful of mint chocolate chip ice cream out of the tub. She had completely sold out. She closed the window. That was it. As of tomorrow, she was free to spend the rest of the summer doing whatever she liked. A few weeks to be a lady of leisure. She gave a sigh of happiness, resting her hand on her belly. It was going to be a wonderful place to bring up their child. She had no idea yet whether it was a boy or a girl, but she didn't mind. It would be a little water baby either way.

Tomorrow she'd be back, lying on a rug, snoozing in the sun. She couldn't wait. She wiped down all the surfaces and put everything away. Then she pulled herself into the driver's seat, stretching the seatbelt over the top of her bump, and drove away, leaving a trail of musical notes drifting across the beach in the late afternoon sun.

TOP TEN
FAVOURITE ICE CREAMS

———————

Magnum

Solero

Mr Whippy 99

Feast

Calippo

Nobbly Bobbly

Fab

Twister

Cornetto

Zoom

Stargazing

She had almost forgotten what it felt like. But now the feeling had come back, she remembered. It was bone-meltingly intoxicating. Her veins fizzed, and there was a corkscrew of lust winding itself deeper and deeper inside her. She could barely breathe, but she needed to, for it was the only way she was going to keep her head and not do something ridiculous. And foolish.

Radar was standing behind her, his arms around her neck, holding his phone in front of her face so they could see the stars and constellations on the screen. He was murmuring their names into her ear.

'Look, there's Orion's Belt. And that's Cassiopeia, in the shape of a W, look.'

'Mmm.' Caroline didn't trust herself to speak. She didn't care one jot about the stars. Not at this very moment, anyway. In general, she agreed they were something to be wondered at. *We are all made of stardust*, she thought, *so it stands to reason we should be fascinated*. And the light pollution here was almost non-existent. The stars shone fierce against the black of the sky. It was spectacular.

But it was nothing in comparison to the shooting stars she felt inside her. She could feel the heat of his body. She couldn't remember the last time she had felt the leanness of youth pressed against her.

Was he teasing her? she wondered. Or did he think she was so old that sex didn't come into it, that he might as well have his arms around a tree trunk? For a moment, she felt tears of self-pity prickle. She was past it. She was never going to make anyone's heart beat faster again.

And then he dropped his head, and she felt his lips on her neck, and he tightened his arms a little. And he gave the smallest sigh, and in it she recognised desire.

She stood still for two more breaths, revelling in the thrill of it all. And then she put up her hands to remove his and stepped away from him.

'Caroline.' His voice was low. 'Oh shit. I didn't mean to offend you.'

She turned to look at him. He looked filled with remorse.

'I just …' Radar stared at her, and she wondered yet again at his beauty, just as she had the day he'd arrived on the steps of the beach hut. 'I … you … I think you're amazing.'

'Me?'

'You're so smart and wise and funny and a total fox.

I didn't mean to be …' He grasped for the right word. 'Inappropriate.'

'Darling, you weren't. I'm very flattered.' She wanted to put him out of his misery. 'And I think you're amazing too. But …' She shook her head. 'I just don't think it's a good idea.'

It had been a funny couple of weeks. Funny because it had been so right. So perfect. They had got on famously. Caroline had written more than she had ever done. She'd had a clarity and a purpose that was on another level, steaming through to the end of what she had now decided would definitely be the last Tuesday adventure. Radar had found his writing mojo too, and they settled into an easy routine: a five-hundred-word warm-up before breakfast, followed by a swim, then coffee and bacon sandwiches while they discussed their writing plans for the day. Then it was a race until lunchtime to see who could write the most. They seemed to take it in turns to win.

Then they had a leisurely lunch while they read what each other had written. Radar would encourage her to be braver, indulge in more wordplay, while she helped him sharpen up and focus what he'd written. They balanced each other well. He benefited from her experience, and she from his willingness to take risks.

'I'm dedicating this book to you,' he grinned at her when she'd made him cut a whole chapter that was stunning writing but digressed from the plot.

'You can save what you've written and use it another time,' she told him.

'Nah. It's going in the bin.' He knew you had to be ruthless to be a really good writer.

Calypso kept phoning to see how they were getting on. Her gamble had paid off. Their fake photo call had hit the headlines, and the publicity had sent their pre-orders through the roof. Their publicists were being bombarded with requests for proofs. They had several interviews lined up with magazines and newspapers. Caroline suddenly found she was being taken seriously, while Radar was the darling of the women's magazines. Their imaginary affair had captured the nation's imagination.

But there was no truth in the rumours, despite what they had led people to believe. Caroline knew it would never work. She would be the one to get hurt if she fell for him. And so she moved away, from his gaze and his grasp.

'I'll make us hot chocolate,' she said, and he sighed.

It was her default setting, to resort to food or drink in order to provide a distraction or cover up her emotions. It had started twenty years ago, during the IVF. Eating gave her comfort every time the treatment didn't work. In the end, her marriage hadn't worked either. Nor had the rebound marriage less than a year later, which only lasted six months. She had felt such a fool, to think that someone wanted her.

That was when she started to write. It was somewhere

to pour her emotions, and a distraction from the fact she felt a failure as a wife and a woman. Did her success make up for that failure? she often wondered. Would she have swapped stardom for a family? Yes, she thought. A million times yes. But she had made the most of the cards she had been dealt. She was not unhappy with her lot. It wasn't the one she would have chosen. But she couldn't, and didn't, complain.

Instead, she'd concentrated on her career – sometimes writing two books a year if the mood took her – and her friends and her love of travel. She didn't need a paramour. She'd had all the romance she needed. She had flings occasionally, usually abroad, little bursts of meaningless pleasure. She was extremely self-sufficient. She didn't *need* anyone else. Or she thought she didn't.

But sometimes lately she longed for the comfort of someone else pottering about in the kitchen, or the warmth of a body in bed next to her. Someone to ask how she had got on at the dentist, or to remind her to get tea bags.

Radar had awoken something else in her. But if she indulged, she knew he would vanish in a puff of smoke afterwards, leaving her with an empty space inside her. He wouldn't give her what she needed. If anything, he would make the longing for companionship even sharper. For she had become fond of him in the last fortnight. She'd enjoyed peeling away the layers. Discovering the

VERONICA HENRY

vulnerable, sensitive, caring man underneath the bad-boy image. He was complex, like the best people always are. Surprising. Contradictory. And funny. She didn't think she had laughed so much in years.

The perfect recipe for heartbreak.

Don't go there, Caroline, she warned herself, as she warmed up a pan of creamy milk and grated half a bar of dark chocolate into it. Then added a slug of Cointreau for good measure. There was nothing that couldn't be made better with liquid chocolate orange. She poured it into two mugs, carefully squirted some cream on top from an aerosol can and grated a little more chocolate over it all. She carried the mugs outside, where Radar was sitting on the steps with his arms around his knees, staring at the sky.

All was quiet, bar the whisper of the waves. It was gone midnight, and everyone in the huts around them had gone to sleep. She sat down next to him and passed him his mug.

'This fortnight,' he said, 'has changed my life.'

'Me too,' she said. 'It's given me the courage to finish things with Tuesday. Try something new and more challenging.'

'I'm not just talking about writing.' He took a sip of his chocolate. There was some cream on his top lip. She longed to kiss it away. She looked out to sea instead. 'I've learned from you that I need to be a better person. You're so wise. And generous. And kind. I've never valued those things before. I've always gone for glitter and glamour. Not that you're not glamorous,' he added hastily, and she smiled. 'But the women I go for never have anything underneath.'

'It's just age, darling. I was shallow and superficial at twenty-five. I didn't know anything. I'm like a good wine. I've mellowed.'

'You're an inspiration.' He turned and looked into her eyes, his gaze steady. 'I think I'm falling in love with you.'

She wanted to laugh, but it would be cruel.

'You're not. I promise you. It's just the novelty. And it would wear off pretty quickly.'

'How do you know? If we don't try?'

She reached out to wipe the cream off his lip. He shivered at her touch. 'I just do,' she said gently.

'Kiss me. I want to know what it would be like to kiss you.'

Caroline couldn't think of anything she'd like to do more. But she knew where kissing would lead. Was it fair on him? Was it fair on her, more to the point? He reached out and rested a wrist on her shoulder, twirling his fingers in her hair, gazing at her.

'It's better left in your head,' she told him. 'In your head, it will be perfect.'

'I want to know,' he insisted, his eyes dark with intensity.

It would be impossible not to give in. Research,

Caroline told herself. It was all in the name of research. She could use this somewhere one day: older woman, younger man. And they were grown-ups. There didn't need to be damage. It was just a physical experience. Like eating oysters or drinking champagne.

He kissed to perfection. The assured kiss of someone who knew how to hint at what might be to come. He tasted of chocolate and Cointreau and his hands were gentle as they entwined themselves in her hair and caressed the back of her neck. Her head was filled with his warm petrichor scent: familiar, earthy. It wakened something primal in her. She wanted their kiss to last forever.

The stars above twinkled with the scandal, blinking on and off in outrage, while the more open-minded sea murmured its approval and the cool night breeze skittered around them, making them pull each other closer.

It would just be a kiss, she reminded herself. That was all. Nothing more.

Just a kiss.

Loaded hot chocolate for unlikely lovers

The perfect nightcap – drink, gaze at the stars and fall in love.

SERVES 2

Full-fat milk
2 tbsp double cream
100g dark chocolate, finely chopped, plus extra for grating
50ml Cointreau, Grand Marnier or King's Ginger
1 × 250g can squirty cream
Ground cinnamon

Fill two mugs three-quarters full with milk and pour into a saucepan. Add the double cream and heat until you see bubbles around the edge of the pan, then turn off the heat and add the chocolate. Stir until the chocolate has melted then add the liqueur of your choice. Pour into the mugs and top with a swirl of squirty cream. Sprinkle with cinnamon and a little grated chocolate. Irresistible!

ACKNOWLEDGEMENTS

Firstly, thank you to Katie Espiner and Sarah Benton for listening to my Negroni-fuelled pitch for this project and making my dream come true.

Massive gratitude to Olivia Barber for her insight, vision and thoughtfulness and helping me make this book the very best it could be.

And as ever my heartfelt appreciation to Harriet Bourton and Araminta Whitley for always being there and catching me when I stumble.

Escape to Everdene Sands, where the sun is shining – but is the tide about to turn?

Robyn and Jake are planning their dream wedding at the family beach hut in Devon. A picnic by the turquoise waves, endless sparkling rosé and dancing barefoot on the golden sand . . .

But Robyn is more unsettled than excited. She can't stop thinking about the box she was given on her eighteenth birthday, and the secrets it contains. Will opening it reveal the truth about her history – and break the hearts of the people she loves most?

As the big day arrives, can everyone let go of the past and step into a bright new future?

Sunshine, cider and family secrets . . .

Dragonfly Farm has been a home and a haven for generations of Melchiors – arch rivals to the Culbones, the wealthy family who live on the other side of the river. Life there is dictated by the seasons and cider-making, and everyone falls under its spell.

For cousins Tabitha and Georgia, it has always been a home from home. When a tragedy befalls their beloved Great-Uncle Matthew, it seems the place where they've always belonged might now belong to them . . .

But the will reveals that a third of the farm has also been left to a Culbone. As the first apples start to fall for the cider harvest, will Dragonfly Farm begin to give up its secrets?

Everyone adores Christmas...

Especially Lizzy Kingham. But this year, she is feeling unloved and under-appreciated by her family. So she wonders . . . what would happen if she ran away and left them to it?

Lizzy heads to her favourite place: a beach hut on the golden sands of Everdene. But back at Pepperpot Cottage, her family are desperate to find her. For Christmas isn't Christmas without Lizzy. Can they track her down in time and convince her she means the world to them, every day of the year?

The perfect mix of family, friends and delicious food.

Laura Griffin is preparing for an empty nest. The thought of Number 11 Lark Hill falling silent – a home usually bustling with noise, people and the fragrant smells of something cooking on the Aga – seems impossible.

Feeling lost, Laura turns to her greatest comfort: her grandmother's recipe box, a treasured collection dating back to the Second World War. Inspired by a bit of the old Blitz spirit, Laura finds a new sense of purpose and her own exciting path to follow.

But even the bravest woman needs the people who love her. And now, they need her in return...

A gorgeous escapist read for anyone needing a hug in a book.

Hunter's Moon is the ultimate 'forever' house. Nestled by a river in the Peasebrook valley, it has been the Willoughbys' home for over fifty years, and now estate agent Belinda Baxter is determined to find the perfect family to live there. But the sale of the house unlocks decades of family secrets – and brings Belinda face to face with her own troubled past . . .

'A delight from start to finish' Jill Mansell

Everyone has a story . . . but will they get the happy ending they deserve?

Emilia has just returned to her idyllic Cotswold hometown to rescue the family business. Nightingale Books is a dream come true for book-lovers, but the best stories aren't just within the pages of the books she sells – Emilia's customers have their own tales to tell.

There's the lady of the manor who is hiding a secret close to her heart; the single dad looking for books to share with his son but who isn't quite what he seems; and the desperately shy chef trying to find the courage to talk to her crush . . .

And as for Emilia's story, can she keep the promise she made to her father and save Nightingale Books?

CREDITS

Veronica Henry and Orion Fiction would like to thank everyone at Orion who worked on the publication of *A Day at the Beach Hut* in the UK.

Editorial
Harriet Bourton
Olivia Barber

Copy editor
Lorraine Jerram

Proof reader
Linda Joyce

Audio
Paul Stark
Amber Bates

Contracts
Anne Goddard
Paul Bulos
Jake Alderson

Design
Rabab Adams
Emily Courdelle
Rosanne Claire
Cooper
Joanna Ridley

Nick May
Helen Ewing
Bryony Clark

**Editorial
Management**
Charlie Panayiotou
Jane Hughes
Alice Davis

Finance
Jasdip Nandra
Afeera Ahmed
Elizabeth Beaumont
Sue Baker

Illustrations
Sarah Corbett

Marketing
Lynsey Sutherland
Helena Fouracre

Production
Ruth Sharvell

Publicity
Maura Wilding
Alainna
Hadjigeorgiou

Sales
Jen Wilson
Esther Waters
Victoria Laws
Rachael Hum
Ellie Kyrke-Smith
Frances Doyle
Georgina Cutler

Operations
Jo Jacobs
Sharon Willis
Lisa Pryde
Lucy Brem